LITERARY ALL-SORTS

A Selection of Stories, Essays and Poems to suit every taste

TABLE OF CONTENTS

WELCOME!

Hello, Reader!

I'm Dorothy. Thank you for dipping into my All-Sorts jar. Feel free to help yourself.

I was born in England over eight decades ago, which makes me pretty ancient, and I came to live in America at the end of 1995. You would think that, after being here for over twenty years, I would have no trouble in understanding my American friends, but that is not always the case. Many words don't convey the same meaning. I'll start this book by describing a few of my experiences.

****

LEARNING THE LINGO

Chatter stopped, and, on either side, I heard breath being sucked between taut lips.

"Dorothy is English," my boss explained to his boss who had just spluttered most of his Merlot onto his rare steak. Around the dinner table, forks hung in mid-air while the rest of the department stared at me, half-shocked, half-amused by what I'd just said.

"Boxes? Really? That's a new one."

The company's Vice President grinned, relieving the tension. He brushed his shirt front with his napkin. A waiter handed him a fresh glass of wine, and laughter and conversation resumed.

"What did I say?" I asked my friend, who sat on my left.

"You did it again," giggled Manuela. She leaned sideways to whisper in my ear. "We *drag* boxes over here. Humping is ... um, um ..."

My cheeks burned. "Not mentioned in polite conversation?"

1

"You've got it."

Americans and English people speak the same language, don't they? Not on your life! The words the Pilgrims spoke when they landed on New England's shores in 1620 had exactly the same meaning as those uttered in Hampshire, England, 3000-odd miles away, but, since then, each State has developed its own special dialects and idioms.

My first exposure to American English came during a visit to the Monterey Aquarium. I was with my daughter (newly married to an American airman) and we were wandering between the huge tanks, looking at the sharks and other marine life, when I saw a sign just ahead that said 'No strollers'.

I stopped dead in my tracks. "Where do we go?" I thought. "We're headed that way and we're definitely strolling."

"Keep going, Mum," my daughter said, treading on my heels.

"I can't. We're not allowed." I pointed to the sign.

Melanie seemed puzzled, and then she laughed. "They mean *pushchairs,* Mum."

That was in 1991. After I settled here in 1995, I found myself bewildered by other differences: not only in word meanings, but in how we live our lives. Here are a few.

Let's start with transport, because that subject is a minefield for the new American. The first thing to get used to, of course, is driving on the opposite side of the road. Oh, and never pass school buses when they are stationary. In England, the only buses are public transport. There, you can pass a bus if you consider it is safe to do so, and it came as a shock to learn that (in most instances) it is illegal here to pass a stationary school bus.

English cars have bonnets and boots, not hoods and trunks. They use tow bars, not hitches, to haul caravans (RVs). You have sedans while we have saloons. English cars drive on the road, but Americans drive on the pavement. That would cause consternation in England because over there a pavement is a footpath, which

2

Americans call a sidewalk. In the glove box, you have a flashlight. We have a torch. I gather that in America, a torch is the equivalent of a fire brand used by Harrison Ford when exploring underground caverns. Lastly, English cars need petrol. Americans abbreviate gasoline to 'gas'. On hearing 'gas' I always think natural gas, and it took me a while to work out how gas mowers work.

My first major embarrassment came when I went to register a used car, (which Americans call previously-owned), and I had to pay for registration plates. In England, the plates stay with the car and are passed from old owner to new owner, vanity plates excepted. If you want vanity plates in England you pay a fortune for the privilege.

The next step was to get my American driving license. After cautiously practising driving in our quiet neighborhood for five weeks, learning the switching sequence of traffic lights, and spending hours swotting up the booklet, I applied for an operator's license.

It was an icy end-of-January day when I ventured onto I93 and headed to downtown Manchester. On the way to the test center situated at the top of a hill, I passed boulders the size of small mountains encased in thick ice. I gripped the wheel with my wooly-gloved hands and shivered in my warm overcoat. But then the sun came out and focused its blaze on my car window. By the time I reached the test center the temperature inside my car was over eighty, my cheeks glowed like ripe pippins, and I sweated profusely, and that was before I anxiously sat down to answer the multi-choice questions.

I don't know what the rules are in other States, but New Hampshire allows three incorrect answers. Well, I got two wrong and one of them was about riding a motor bike. The examiner looked at my wrinkles, smiled indulgently and said, "I guess you don't have to lose any sleep about that one, ma'am." Then he handed me a slip of paper and directed me to the queue (or line) of people waiting to have their photographs taken.

He was very friendly and approachable, so I decided to ask him about one of the questions that really bothered me.

"Excuse me," I said. "Can you tell me why I had to answer that question about the tractor? I mean, this is hardly a rural area."

He picked up my answer sheet. "Which question, ma'am?" He trailed his finger down the sheet until I told him to stop. He frowned. "You got that right. What's the problem?"

I bit my finger nail. "Are tractors and trailers actually allowed on main roads over here? In the middle of a city?"

He stared at me, not understanding immediately, but then comprehension dawned. "Ah, by tractor, are you thinking, um, John Deere?"

"Never heard of a John Deere. Where I come from they're Massey Fergusons."

He frowned again. "And the trailer?"

"A cultivator, reaper. Those things are so WIDE."

He put down my answer sheet and came round my side of his desk. With a fatherly arm around my shoulders (although I must have been his senior by at least two decades) he led me to the window and pointed to a huge vehicle that was grinding its gears as it struggled up a slope leading off I93. He patted my shoulder.

"What do you call that, ma'am?"

"An articulated lorry. Right?"

He shook his head.

"Oh, I know what it is," I said, clicking my fingers while I sought the word I wanted. "It's a, a pantechnicon!"

He shook his head again.

I couldn't believe him. With my mouth a perfect O, I said "No-o-o-o-o-o?"

"No, ma'am." He patted my shoulder again and whispered, "Tractor trailer."

Now both my eyes and my mouth were perfect Os.

We turned away from the window. "Go get your picture taken," he said.

A few minutes later, with the small card clutched in my hand, I made my way to the door. My friendly examiner looked up and smiled. I returned the smile, and then looked out of the window. Another huge truck was negotiating the steep I93 exit. I pointed to it.

"Tractor trailer," I burbled.

He game me another smile and a thumbs-up. "You've got it," he said.

Enough of cars and driving. Let's go indoors.

No, no, wait a sec. Imagine we are standing outside a pair of houses. You would call them duplexes. In England, they are semi-detached. We enter the house via the front door on the ground floor, which to you is the first floor. Then we go upstairs and, in England, would be on the first floor, while Americans insist it's the second floor. So, no matter how tall the building, Brits and Yanks are always one storey/story out of synch. Of course, in any building, Americans use elevators while the English go up in a lift.

That reminds me, we give hitchhikers a lift along the road while you give them a ride.

Okay, let's go back indoors. Brits have cupboards in the kitchen and wardrobes in the bedroom, while Americans have closets. In either room, you flick the switch up to turn the light on. Brits flick it down. Your globes screw into place. English bulbs have a bayonet cap. We push the prongs up into the lampholder and twist the bulb left or right so that the prongs drop into slots. The first time I changed a light bulb here, I must have screwed it in the wrong direction because the whole fitting fell onto my head.

When we are in the bathroom, I turn on the tap while you use the faucet. I wash my face with a flannel, but my son-in-law uses a washcloth. If he cuts himself shaving, he sticks on a Band Aid. Brits use a plaster or a bit of toilet paper. When out shopping, if I need to spend a penny, I look for a toilet or a loo, but Americans seek a restroom. Restroom! A restroom should be a peaceful, quiet place, a hushed haven where you can doze or read, or have a cup of tea. Definitely not what WalMart offers on a busy weekend, or on any day, come to think of it.

When applying for my first job in America, I found that, here again, words had different meanings. I was surprised to be told that instead of being paid, I would receive compensation. What? In England compensation is given to remedy a wrong, like when a person is injured or property is spoiled.

When asked about my previous experience I said I'd left all my jobs voluntarily, except once when I'd been made redundant.

"You can't be *made* redundant," the interviewer said. "Either you are redundant, or you aren't."

"I still lost my job," I countered. "Not as bad as being given the sack or being fired."

Her eyebrows rose. "Here we would let you go, or give you a pink slip."

I shook my head in confusion. "Let me go? That suggests a choice. And what the heck has ladies' underwear to do with losing a job?"

She laughed. "I wasn't talking about intimate apparel. In the old days, companies gave their workers a pink piece of paper when their employment ceased, and we still use the phrase."

"I see. A bit like being given your cards?"

"You've got it."

Food is a well-known area where words mean different things. Cookies are the equivalent of our biscuits, but your biscuits are our scones. Your muffins are delicious little cakes, while our muffins are thick crumpets. Our crisps are potato snacks, which you call chips. We buy chips smothered in salt and vinegar from the chippie, along with fillets of fish. Our sweets are your candy and our regular coffee comes hot, to which we add cream and sugar. I never had iced tea or coffee before I came here.

Then there are sandwiches. Let me make you an English salad sandwich. I take two slices of bread, and butter them. Then, onto one slice, I add lettuce, tomato, cucumber, thinly sliced onion, and hard-boiled egg. After seasoning with salt, pepper, and a squirt of salad cream, I place the other slice of bread over the loaded slice, pat it down with my hand and make a diagonal cut, before offering the sandwich to you on a pretty china plate.

I'd only been in the States a week when my son-in-law offered to buy me a sandwich. What kind did I want? The board listed egg salad, tuna salad, and BLT. I plumped for egg salad, expecting something similar to what I've just described. Instead, I was given half a loaf of bread filled with a squishy egg and mayonnaise concoction that dripped everywhere. But – as you would say – Man, it was goooood!

Nowadays, I don't make so many faux pas, but my daughter-in-law still shakes her head when I call somebody 'homely', intending it as a compliment. It appears that I still have some way to go before I have finally learned the lingo.

****

I joined a temping agency as soon as I'd mastered using Windows instead of WorkPerfect. Oh, dear. I felt like a first-year student. And I had to learn Excel, too. I loved its autosum feature. The agency placed me at a retirement fund investment firm and I learned a new meaning for the initials I R A. I spent five years at that firm, and loved every minute, but then left to look after three prematurely born grandchildren. They were happy years, too.

However, I had bills to pay and landed a weekend job as a Greeter at WalMart. From being a Greeter I progressed to being a cashier and would probably still work there if bad health had not intervened. After leaving WalMart, I wrote short stories in my spare moments. Here's a humorous story, prompted by my ten years working at WalMart.

****

WAR AT WALMART

Dave Smith threw down his pen in disgust. His story, *War at WalMart*, was turning out to be a farce. Not the dramatic account, full of fire and fury, that he intended it to be.

That wild fight seemed such a promising subject. He'd been there, had taken part in it, but he hadn't started it. That cocky Lou Martin had started it by picking on Simon again, just because Simon can't tell a zucchini from a cucumber. But you put Simon in the apples and he'll sort out the Galas from the Grannies in no time.

Dave read what he'd written so far. He liked alliteration and had used it deliberately when describing the flying fruit, the shredding and scattering of the large limp lettuces when they'd been tossed among the turnips and taters and tomatoes. He frowned. Perhaps he shouldn't have written 'taters' but it went so well with the turnips and tomatoes. And he was pleased with his ballet of the bananas – the way he'd described the over-ripe fruit flying onto the floor, and associates and customers alike skidding on the skins and careening around the counters like ice skaters.

He nibbled the end of his pen while recalling the scene. Everyone in Produce had grabbed grapes or plump plums and had pelted Lou, forcing him to flee into Deli/Bakery, right next to Produce, where he'd hidden behind the rotisseries. Dave couldn't remember who had flung the first frosted cake, but it had landed on Miss Sue-Ellen's head just as she was weighing up wedges at the hot food counter.

Someone reported the fracas to the Fitting Room. Latoya shouted over the loudspeaker: "Management to Produce." That broke up the weekly staff meeting and Manager Antonio hauled Lou and Simon into the Admin Office. How Dave wished he could've been a fly on the wall. They say Antonio has a way with words when he's angry – a blistering, make-you-wish-you'd-never-been-born kind of way.

While that dressing-down was going on, the rest of the stock in Produce was tossed into the parking lot so the floor could be hosed down. Customers had a field day. They took everything, down to the last shallot.

Dave rested his head in his hands. The deadline for this competition was December 1st. He looked at the clock. Eleven-thirty. Oh boy, was he tired, but he had to finish the story before going to bed. He massaged his forehead and tried to find the words, the perfect words, that Simon could plead to Antonio, justifying his retaliation to Lou's teasing.

The room started spinning and Dave felt himself hurtling through the night over a strange city. Then he was falling, falling, falling into a dark courtyard. Creepy vines reached for him and pulled him into an alcove at the back of which was a door. He turned the knob, crept in and found himself at the foot of a spiral staircase that led up to a shadowy, shelf-filled room, very much like an old library. Instead of books, however, the shelves held thousands of small dispensers, each bearing the name of a famous person, every one of them dead.

An old woman sat at a desk near the entrance. She waved to Dave, as if she knew him.

"Hey, there. You again? What are you after this time?"

"Drama. Something really brilliant and unforgettable."

She cocked a thumb towards the end of the room. "Vintage is over there. Go easy on the lever. You only need a dab, you know."

It was a long walk to the Vintage section, and the walls of the room seemed to squeeze in on him. Other people were working there, and it was difficult to get by them, especially one man who was fat and had a habit of dodging backwards and forwards. Eventually Dave found the A section. It started with Aaron and ended with Azimov. Impatiently he made his way past the Bs, Cs, and Ds, while being constantly dogged by the fat man.

Eventually he reached S – his goal, and searched for the dispenser he wanted. He looked to see if the woman was watching him, but the fat man was blocking her view. Furtively, Dave pushed the lever on the dispenser and let his palm fill with cool, clear oil. It ran down his neck and onto his arms when he massaged his scalp, and he had to rub his hands on his pants to get rid of the excess.

He ran back to the staircase which had turned into a slide. He found himself sliding down it on his backside, wind whistling through his hair, as he plunged down, down, down ...

His head hit against something hard. He opened his eyes to find himself sprawled across his desk just as the clock in the hall bonged twelve.

Midnight! He must have dropped off.

"Better get this story finished and go to bed," he told himself.

He picked up his pen and started putting words into Simon's mouth.

"Senor Antonio,

Many a time, and oft in Produce, Lou has berated me about being clumsy and my uselessness. Still have I borne it like a stupid mug

Until today..."

****

All too soon, the hectic days of infant childcare ended – no more quiet time between one p.m. and two p.m. when I would read a *Magic Tree House* chap book to my three little terrors before settling them down for a nap on the carpet. I had leisure time and found myself writing more.

My blue minivan joined the stream of other vehicles, morning and mid-afternoon, when I took the grandkids to school or collected them from it. I became involved in homework, sports events, and Christmas plays. One such production led me to write the following story, and I kid you not. One little daredevil did glide across the stage wearing his Heeleys! (Do you remember Heeleys? They were sneakers with wheels in their heels.)

****

JACK IN THE BOX

The make-shift curtains closed jerkily, but not before a kindergartner dodged in front of them and squinted into the darkness, apparently unaware of the three-foot drop immediately in front of him. A curtain-puller leaned out and yanked him back to safety. Still waving and smiling, the little lad disappeared behind the blue material.

There was no sound on stage for several minutes, and the audience began whispering and laughing. Then noisy scampering on stage told Traci that her nineteen first-graders were taking their places for the last performance in the Christmas concert.

"Are you all right, Jack?" she whispered into her walkie-talkie.

11

Silence.

"Turn your mike on, Jack," she urged.

A timid "Got it, miss," answered her.

"Just sit still up there and do your best. Okay?"

"Yes, miss."

"Ready?" asked Ian, the art teacher who sat next to her, his fingers poised over the tape recorder.

Traci gulped and nodded. "Please, please God, don't let anything go wrong," she prayed.

So many things had gone wrong in the few weeks since she'd started teaching at this private school: misunderstandings over rules, nasty notes from parents after she'd made a typo in one of her letters – and it **was** a typo. Of course she knew how to spell 'pigeon'. She'd had trouble getting to school on time and, on top of that, there was Jack. Clumsy, noisy, ever-eager-to-please Jack with his inability to sit still and his impish grin that made him her favorite. She knew she shouldn't have favorites but he reminded her so much of her own brother when he was that age. No, it wasn't Jack. It was Jack's viper-tongued mother. Traci had clashed with some of the other mothers but they hadn't caused her to seek refuge in the bathroom where she had shed tears, or made her feel stupid, a complete dummy, the way Jack's mother had.

The curtains swished open to reveal her class. The front row of six, mostly boys, knelt on stage. They had tinsel wrapped around their foreheads and waved silver stars. Some of the headdresses were already drifting apart, and one little urchin crossed his eyes while he blew a loose end into the air.

Behind the star-wavers stood six fidgeting girls dressed in yellow. The girl in the middle, the most restless of all, caught everyone's attention in her gold, voluminous tulle creation that sparkled with light-catching sequins.

The middle level of the bleachers held six boys and an equal number of girls wearing simple white tunics. They had paper flames sprouting from their heads and were supposed to be candles.

And Jack? Jack was squatting in a big cardboard box on the top tier of the bleachers. The open side of the box had been turned towards the audience. A decorator's ladder, right behind the bleachers, made a wider platform for the box to rest on. The ladder was duct-taped to the bleachers, and the box was taped to both bleachers and ladder to make it safe.

Traci had fixed several tap lights (the kind you stick in the pantry or at the bottom of the stairs) around the inside of the box. Jack had to tap the lights gently to illuminate his cave. Traci crossed her fingers and prayed that he wouldn't touch them before he was supposed to.

During rehearsals, Jack had been the only kid who'd had the nerve to climb into the box, and if he sat still he would be perfectly safe. But Jack was a fidget. If he leaned too much to one side, if he shuffled back too far – Traci trembled at the thought of what Jack's mother would do if her precious son tumbled, and she crossed her fingers again.

Ian's finger pressed the power button and the tinsel-headed children seemed to sing *"If I were a beautiful twinkling star, I'd shine on the darkest night"*. Two of them sat motionless, not even moving their lips, but the other four waved their stars and tried to sing along with the recording. At the end of their song, they scampered to the side of the stage.

Then the yellow-clad girls stepped forward and sang, *"Jesus wants me for a sunbeam"*. With the other little girls swaying behind her, the lead Sunbeam pranced to and fro, leaping and bowing left and right, revealing her lace-edged panties. She acknowledged each indulgent laugh from the audience with a little smirk. After *"I'll be a sunbeam for him"* rang out for the last time, she reluctantly sat down and the spotlight turned to the Candles, each of whom waved a battery-powered Christmas candle aloft.

Traci's hands sweated and she squeezed a tissue in her palms. So far, so good, but here came the test.

At her signal, all the lights – on stage and off – dimmed, and the tiny candles bobbed and tilted in the darkness. *"Jesus bids us shine"* began weakly, and Ian turned the volume up. After the words *"You in your small corner..."* he stopped the tape. Silence reigned for a few seconds. Then the box illuminated as Jack punched two of the lights. When he reached towards more lights, his knees extinguished the bottom ones and the box went black again. In a panic, he hit out at the lights wildly. They flashed on and off like strobe lights at a disco while he squirmed about.

"Sorry, miss." Jack's tear-laden cry carried through the microphone.

"It's all right, Jack," Traci soothed. "Sing your line."

"And I in mine," wept Jack.

Sympathetic laughter rippled around the hall. That wasn't the effect Traci wanted.

Ian jabbed the button again and the Candles plunged into their second verse. Traci sank onto her chair, disappointed and trembling. Her smooth dark hair curtained her hands as she rested her face in her palms. It was her fault. She had expected too much of Jack. She hadn't been thinking of him at all, about how he could be hurt, physically and mentally.

Oh, Jack. I'm so sorry.

When the singers reached *"You in your small corner..."* again, there was another pause. A much longer pause. Traci peeped unwillingly through her fingers. Slowly, as Jack tapped the lights in turn round the box, it lit up. Then he sat quietly, arms stretched above his head, eyes closed as if blissfully content. The lights gleamed on his face and then, sweetly, unbelievably sweetly, Jack sang *"And I in mine."*

There was no laughter this time. No sound at all – until the clapping started. It went on and on, until the Headmaster stood and signaled for it to stop.

The hall lights came on and conversation buzzed while Traci's class formed a semi-circle on stage and watched Jack climb down from his perch. He ignored the hands stretched out to him and nearly came a cropper when he jumped the last two levels of the bleachers.

The children filed slowly off stage, not looking where they were going because they were seeking the wave, the call, that told them where their parents had positioned themselves. Jack seemed to glide off. How? Then it dawned on Traci. So help her, the little tyke was wearing his Heeleys. And he'd jumped down from the bleachers. He could've broken his leg – or his neck.

Chairs scraped, and parents packed their cameras and phones away. Some crept towards the exits, not waiting for the Head's final address and prayers.

Traci bowed her head, but heard nothing. It had gone right after all. "Thank you, Jack," she breathed, blowing her nose into an already soggy tissue.

While the rows of chairs were cleared from the body of the hall, the teachers manned tables set along the sides. Traci was grateful that her table was the farthest from the stage. She was still trembling from the ordeal and needed time to compose herself. She fiddled with the plates of cookies, set out rows of paper cups and placed napkins at each corner.

Ian had gone backstage to uncouple the box. What should she do with that? She could use a couple of the tap lights, but not ten of them. Looking across the hall, she saw a mother making a beeline towards her, dragging a pouting Sunbeam, while Jack and his mother were headed her way, too. Then Sunbeam's mother saw Jack and put on a spurt.

Traci greeted Mrs. Sunbeam before she asked, "What's the matter?"

"I wanted to be in the box," pouted the girl.

"She'd have made a much better job of it," her mother agreed.

"But you were our sunbeam!" gasped Traci. There was no pleasing some people. "What would we have done without your dance, and that beautiful dress?"

Mrs. Sunbeam preened. "It took me hours," and she launched into a description of how much material it had taken, the number of sequins she'd sown on, and how much it had cost.

Her words flowed on and on. Would she never stop? Traci caught Jack's eye. He and his mother waited patiently a few feet away. Then Mrs. Sunbeam said, "And Carla practiced that dance over and over, making sure she got it right."

Traci took a chance. "Now, if she could put as much dedication into her writing," she said, laughing to soften the criticism.

"We're working on it," retorted Mrs. Sunbeam, clearly annoyed. "Oh, look, Carla. There's Jordan's mother talking to the Head. Let's show her your dress."

They stomped away and Jack's mother moved forward.

Traci's hand shook as she tucked a strand of hair behind her ear, and she forced a smile. "H-hello," she said, her voice suddenly husky.

Jack's mother was looking down at her son. She seemed to be having trouble deciding what to say. She darted a quick glance at Traci, before she blurted, "M-my Jack." Her chin quivered and Traci saw her gulp. "M-my Jack," she said again. "My Jack's never been a s-s-star b-before. You made him a star!" She looked straight at Traci, her eyes bright with proud tears. One escaped and she turned to dab it away.

Traci pressed her lips together in an effort to stop them trembling, and she tried to think of a reply. Her words, however, were impeded by the lump in her throat. She felt a tear slide down her cheek and she dashed it away with the back of her hand. Swallowing hard, she managed to say "And he didn't let me down."

The two women exchanged watery smiles. Traci grabbed one of the paper napkins and blew hard into it. Jack's mother reached for one, too, and blotted her eyes.

"Mom, mom," Jack tugged at his mother's free hand. "Don't forget to ask..."

She interrupted him. "No. You ask, Jack."

The little boy looked anxiously at Traci. "Please, miss, please can I have the box?"

Traci hadn't expected that. She spread her hands. "Yes, if you want it. But how will you get it home? It's heavy and awkward."

Traci looked around for Ian. He was making his way towards them, the box on his shoulder. "What are you going to do with this?" he asked.

"I'm giving it to Jack."

Jack's face lit up and he reached for the box. "I wanna put it over my head, 'cept I'd need a hole to put my head through. An', an' holes in the sides for my arms. Like Sponge Bob."

Ian grinned and pulled out his penknife. "Now, just where do you want these holes?"

Teacher and parent watched Ian cut holes and then lift the box over the eager youngster.

"Thank you. Thank you so much." Jack's mother offered a tentative hand.

Traci gripped the hand and squeezed it. "You're welcome."

They smiled at each other, and then Jack started marching towards the exit. Other children ran towards him.

"Is that yours, Jack?" "Cor, giss a go!"

"I don't know how we'll get him in the car," Jack's mother said. "I'd better go help him. Thank you again."

Traci and Ian watched them leave.

"Well, that went off pretty well," Ian said. "What a surprise."

"Yes it was." Traci rubbed her chin. "But, come to think of it, it's just what you'd expect from a Jack-in-the-box."

****

Traci's story makes me jump onto my soapbox. I pride myself on my spelling and I cringe when I see mistakes in publications which should have been properly proofed before being sold or, worse, in leaflets coming home from schools. Hence the following essay:

SPELLBOUND

I have a terrible affliction. I am plagued by spelling mistakes and grammatical errors. They come at me from every direction – leaping off pages (paper and electronic) like pesky fleas, harassing me from hoardings and taunting me from televisions. Swarms of its/it's and lies/lays get in my hair, while bigger errors slap me in the face. Most of the time I suffer in silence, emitting nothing more than a low growl while baring my teeth which, to the casual observer, could be attributed to a sudden bout of heartburn.

But when it comes to books that should have been proofread before leaving the publisher, I take up my cudgels.

In *Treasure of Khan*, I found myself confronted by a **heard** of thirsty camels. I kid you not. It's there in black and white on page 158. On page 283, guards on horses, and then Pitt and Giordino on a motor cycle, make **decents** down a mountain. And to make matters worse, on the next page more horses start an **ascent down** the mountain! I wrote to the publisher pointing out thirteen errors all told, expecting to receive an apology, but so far not a peep. I wonder if my letter even reached the Senior Vice President, Publisher and Editor in Chief (the same person holding all those rôles) or whether it went straight into the waste paper basket.

In Chapter 2 of *Leapholes*, Ryan hits his **breaks** (while riding a bike) and, on page 178, he puts his foot on the bottom **wrung** of a ladder. Chapters 9 and 12 start with **Rhe** (in spite of a large dropped capital letter which should have been easy to spot) and Chapter 23 begins **Rever** (same comment). Since seventeen of the thirty-seven chapters start with "Ryan" I wonder if the typesetter got into a groove, or had a job lot of capital Rs to use up. I wonder, too, if it was one of his ancestors who first coined the phrase: 'the three Rs'.

I bought an educational place mat from WalMart, thinking that my 7-year-old grandson could learn something useful while eating dinner, instead of flicking peas at his sister, but I have never used it. Why not? Because slap dab in the middle of it lies the **Astroid** Belt. Greenbrier/ Scentex got it right on the back. Why didn't they check the front?

Schools are far from exempt, private or public.

A handwriting exercise from my grandson's expensive private school, made me cross. He had to practice writing the alphabet. Each letter had its own verse. The one for X was:

Xx is an Example exhibiting, on **it's** side,
a little picture of the cross where Jesus bled and died.

What chance does this boy have of getting its/it's right if he's taught wrongly in first grade?

The same boy later attended a public school. I had to collect him after drama group one day and waited in the foyer. A huge poster caught my eye. In letters at least two inches high it heralded a forthcoming Golf **Tournemant**.

I squirmed. Hadn't the poster's creator used Spellcheck? How many posters had been printed? There were several weeks to go before the event took place. Maybe more posters could be printed, and this dreadful spelling mistake – in a school, no less – (I couldn't get over that), could be tactfully withdrawn. That would surely save the author from embarrassing comments. With hope in my heart, I called the contact number at the bottom of the poster. A man picked up straight away.

"Excuse me," I started. "Could you please tell me who made the big poster hanging in the XYZ school foyer?"

"I did," he responded, proudly.

"Um. Are you aware that there are two spelling mistakes in the heading?"

"Oh, are there? So.....?"

"This poster is in a *school*."

"What's that got to do with it?"

"Wouldn't it be best to correct it?"

"What for?" He sounded irritated. "Everyone knows what I mean."

It was my turn to be irritated. He obviously wasn't at all bothered by his bad spelling, so I said goodbye. A couple of weeks later, when I visited the school again, the poster still hung in its prominent position, taunting me about the now-imminent **Tournemant.**

What would you do if you were me? I thought about going to the doctor for help with my affliction, but I dare say he would tell me to get a life and charge me a hefty fee.

I guess I'll just have to live with it.

****

My grandchildren, all born prematurely, were Irish triplets. The eldest was born in 2000 and his twin siblings came along in 2001, arriving six weeks before the eldest had his first birthday. Taking them all out at once was, to say the least, difficult, but they loved going to the store, especially WalMart, and for a while they could all sit in one cart while I pushed it around, shopping for necessities. My big fear was that one of them would have a melt-down, like so many other kids did, but I was spared that embarrassment.

Later, the fear of a melt-down became small beer when compared with the panic of losing one of them. You know, kids can be as slippery as eels, no matter how closely you watch them. One day, I saw a boy (eight or nine years old) put in charge of his bratty little brother while Mom used the restroom, and I wrote the following story as a result.

MY BROTHER'S A BRAT

The noise of the passing siren filled the room and drowned what Big Bird was saying on the television. Two-and-a-half-year-old Jackson ran to Mom and hid his face in her lap, while ten-year-old Brad looked out the window until the flashing light was out of sight. Then he returned to the table and concentrated on building his model.

"Simon, simon," Jackson wailed.

"It's all right, honey," Mom said, gently stroking his hair. "The police car is going to help someone. The siren tells the other cars to get out of the way. We've told you that over and over, haven't we?"

Jackson looked fearfully towards the window. Faintly, but quickly getting louder, came the harsh, impatient honk of a fire engine.

"There'll be an ambulance next," Brad predicted. He went back to the window. Their house stood on a corner which was governed by traffic lights.

"Told you!"

The fire engine swept past, followed by an ambulance, its light flashing and bell clanging. Both vehicles were headed for the busy intersection two miles up the road.

"Simons. Don't like simons." Jackson still clung to Mom.

"I know you don't, honey," Mom said. She lifted the toddler onto her knee. "But they won't hurt you. They won't come here. They're too busy getting to that person who needs help. Look at the TV. They're trying to find Ernie. Where do you think he is?"

Jackson watched for a few minutes before he squirmed down onto the rug and started pushing his toy car, loudly imitating the last siren.

"Do you **have** to make that noise?" Brad asked.

"Hush, honey. He's only playing," Mom scolded, but she gave the toddler a short swat on the butt and warned him. "Inside voice, honey. If you want to yell, go out in the yard."

"Bwad play with me," Jackson demanded. He grabbed hold of the table leg and jerked it. A chunk of Brad's model collapsed.

"Now look what you've done! You spoil everything, you ...."

Brad wanted to call his little brother something he shouldn't, but Mom was eyeing him sternly and Dad came in from the kitchen to see what was going on.

"It's not fair. He never gets told off," Brad grumbled.

"You're right. It's not fair, son," Dad said. "But you're a big boy and you can handle it. Will you give him some time on his swing? It's nice outside and he loves playing with you."

Brad looked longingly at his model.

"It's nearly nap time," Mom said, "and then you can build in peace."

"I guess. Come on, brat!"

"Wing? Bwad push me on wing?"

"When's he gonna talk proper?"

"Soon, honey. He won't be a baby much longer."

--o--

Mom went to the back door with the two boys and watched them cross the grass to the swing. She turned to speak to Dad. "We had it too easy with Brad," she sighed. "He was so good. Never defied me the way Jackson does."

Dad smiled. "But Brad had his moments, too. Remember when he broke his arm climbing? And when he fell in the fish pond?"

"Just as well you filled it in. Jackson would've had a ball, going after the fish. And to think we were worried he wouldn't make it. Six weeks preemie and not even three pounds."

"Nothing wrong with him now, but he sure is a handful."

"You can say that again, honey."

--o--

Outside, Brad helped Jackson scramble into the swing, and then bent to clip the harness.

"Me do it."

"You can't."

"Why?"

"You're too little. You can't press the black bits hard enough."

"Can, so."

"No, you can't. Get your hand out of the way. Let me do it."

Jackson kicked Brad, and started to scream.

"Do you want me to push you or not?"

Jackson nodded.

"Then stop yelling and let me fix the straps."

24

Brad untangled the harness. He was about to push one plastic tab in place when a loud bang and a crunching noise came from the main road at the front of the house. A scream pierced the air, followed by more bangs and squealing brakes.

Jackson slid off the swing and darted towards the fence surrounding their play area. Brad chased him but his little brother squeezed through a gap between the fence and a prickly bush. He ran down the long, narrow, unfenced stretch of grass at the side of the house, towards the road, laughing and squealing in glee.

Brad sped after him. The bush scraped his face and arms when he crashed through it, and Jackson was only feet from the road when Brad caught hold of his brother's shirt and yanked him to a stop.

"Leggo. Leggo."

"No."

Brad had seen enough to know that something horrible had happened at the lights. He wrapped his arms around the wriggling, kicking toddler and dragged him back to the yard, watched by his parents at the lounge window. Mom's eyes and mouth were rounded in horror. Dad had a phone to his mouth. While Brad struggled to drop Jackson to safety over the fence, his little brother's fists and feet pummeled him.

"Stay there!" he bawled at the screaming child before he squeezed back through the bush. Blood trickled down his neck and he felt sore all over.

"Oh, my God! Come inside, both of you!"

Mom came running across the grass. She scooped up Jackson and cradled his head into her shoulder, while sobbing "Oh, my baby, my baby. Are you hurt?"

She went back to the house. Brad limped painfully after her, but didn't go in. He sat on the back steps and rubbed his arms and legs, sore on the inside, too. Mom wasn't bothered about him. Just Jackson. He felt sad and angry, and unwanted.

"Come indoors, Brad." Mom stood right behind him.

"I want to stay here." Brad wiped his streaming nose on his bare arm.

"Come inside, honey. Thank God you were with him, and you caught him. Oh, jeez, you're bleeding. Come in, honey, and let me fix that."

She helped Brad to stand, put a protective arm around his shoulder, and led him into the kitchen where she ran warm water into a small bowl. While she gently dabbed at the stinging scratches, Brad began to feel better.

Outside, sirens wailed and red and blue lights flashed among a mess of vehicles where paramedics bent over two figures, hidden under blankets. One of the police cars reversed into their driveway, its blue light throbbing.

Jackson whimpered "Simon, simon," until Mom picked him up and comforted him.

The front door bell rang, and Brad heard voices.

"Who's Dad talking to?"

"The police, honey. One of those cars ran through the light and ploughed into the other. They're asking for witnesses."

"Jackie won't believe you now."

"What do you mean?"

"You told him sirens wouldn't come here, but there's one right by the door."

Mom gasped. "I never dreamed this would happen," she said.

Dad invited the policemen into the lounge so they could view the scene from a new angle, but he insisted none of them had seen the accident happen. Mom cuddled Jackson tight and then sat down heavily on the couch. When Brad climbed up beside her, she put an arm round him and held him close.

After the ambulances drove away and photographs had been taken, the police got traffic moving again and the intersection finally settled down to normal working. Then the last police car drove off.

"Simon gone now?" whispered Jackson. He looked at Brad, and then at the window.

"Yes. All gone. Scaredy cat."

"Hush, honey. That's not nice," Mom said.

Brad scowled. "He's a mini moanysaurus. He's a pain."

Jackson threw a toy at Brad, and climbed back on Mom's knee.

"We should get you a siren," Dad suggested. "Then, if you're in a jam any time, you can turn it on and we'll come and help you."

"Simon help Jackie?"

"Sure, kiddo."

Brad had bad dreams that night. He kept remembering the way his heart had lurched when he saw his baby brother running towards the road, how the bush had held him up by spreading its prickly arms, and all the while, in the background, sirens sighed and lights flashed.

Jackson, though, had a good night's sleep and woke early, demanding strawberry milk and Fruit Loops.

On the way home from work the next day, Dad stopped by a store and bought Jackson a set of emergency vehicles, each having a different siren. He bought Brad another building kit and a new computer game, so that Brad didn't feel left out. Jackson played with his noisy new toys all the time and took them everywhere with him.

--o--

A few weeks after the accident outside their house, Mom took Brad and Jackson to a huge mall to start Christmas shopping. The aisles were packed and Mom kept Jackson strapped in the seat of the cart until he clutched his shorts and demanded the potty. Mom needed to go, too. It took ages to reach the restroom, and when they finally got there, Mom lifted Jackson down and asked Brad to wait outside and watch their cart.

Jackson had left his ambulance on the seat and Brad idly pushed it round and round on its front wheels so the siren didn't engage. Ten minutes passed and Brad got bored. There must be loads of people in there, he thought. He dropped the toy ambulance in his pocket and leaned against the cart. Just then a familiar giggle made him look up. He saw Jackson scamper off, head down, into the legs of people, the way he did at home. Mom was trying to leave the restroom while other people were pushing their way in.

Mom shouted "Jackson! Jackson!" but the toddler had disappeared.

"I'll get him, Mom. I saw where he went."

Brad headed towards the spot where he thought his brother had gone, but he wasn't there. He ran down each aisle, bobbing up and down, looking either for Jackson's unruly blond hair or his white sneakers that had twinkling lights. He, too, called "Jackson! Jackson!" but announcements over the paging system drowned him out. Then he remembered the toy in his pocket. He spun the back wheels and held the ambulance over his head.

"Wheee-eee-eee! Waa wa wa wa wa!"

Shoppers turned in surprise and moved quickly out of his way.

"Who are you looking for?" a tall woman asked, seeing the concern on Brad's face.

"My little brother. He's only two. Got a red shirt on."

The woman pivoted slowly, scanning the area. "Is that him?" she asked.

She pointed to a display of popcorn and candy outside the small cafeteria. Jackson stood there, twisting his tee shirt in his chubby hands, his eyes wide with fright as he looked for someone he knew. He screwed up his face and Brad knew he would soon be bawling.

"Yeah! That's him. Thanks."

Brad sprinted towards the display. He spun the wheels on the toy again and lifted it high.

Jackson heard the wail and began jumping up and down in anticipation, a big smile on his face, replacing the tears. Then he saw Brad, ran to him, and grabbed hold of Brad's legs.

"My simon. My simon. Gimme my simon. Where's Mommy? I wan' Mommy."

"She's coming. Why did you run off like that, you midgie monster?"

"Gimme my simon."

"You can have it when we get back to Mom. Hold my hand."

"No."

Jackson plonked himself on the floor and refused to budge.

"Aw, come on, Jackie. I'll give you a piggie back."

The smile came back and the toddler grabbed Brad's neck. "Piggie back, piggie back," he chanted.

Brad bumped Jackson as high as he could on his back. "Here, take your simon, er, siren, and make it work so Mom can hear. She's over there. See her?"

Brad pointed to an aisle where he could see his mother frantically looking every which way, seeking them. The toy's siren blasted into his ear, making him cringe. He felt Jackson slipping, but managed to hold him until he reached Mom, when he dropped him on the floor.

Mom strapped Jackson firmly into the cart. He gave her an angelic smile and set the siren working again.

"You've got a smart youngster there, ma'am."

The tall lady stopped beside Mom and they both watched Jackson zoom the toy into a death-defying plunge.

"Yes. I know."

Brad turned away. His little brother did dumb things all the time, but everyone thought he was so smart. Then, to his surprise, Mom's arm snuck round his shoulder. He looked up to see her smiling at him.

"He's the smartest kid ever. What would I do without you, honey?"

Brad's eyes sparkled and he couldn't help smiling back, but then he shrugged his shoulders. "No big deal. You'd have found him," he said, as if it didn't matter. But it did and his heart sang.

"Was I a pain when I was little?" he asked.

"You were never a brat, honey, which makes coping with Jackson so hard. I'm glad I have you to help me. Come on, let's go home and hide our Christmas parcels before Dad sees them. He's as bad as Jackson at trying to find them."

****

An early assignment in the course I took with LongRidge was to write a short story, under 1500 words, about employment. I'd been an office worker all my working career, except for the weekends at WalMart, so I chose to write about the anxious days when I was a temp. It was always a relief when I was asked to come back for another week. Here's my assignment: part true, part fiction.

****

ADAM'S APPLE

Donna put her car in reverse, ready to leave the parking lot, when she remembered the apple. She dithered whether to go back and retrieve it, or leave it behind at Faith Investments, together with her hopes of finding a permanent job there. It would have been ideal. So near home. Temping was okay to bring in extra pennies while Phil was the main breadwinner, but not since he'd walked out on her and Vicky.

Mustn't think of Phil.

For the last five days she'd struggled with unfamiliar software and new procedures and thought she'd coped pretty well, but she hadn't been asked to come back, and Charles Bristow, for whom she'd been working, hadn't even said goodbye.

But Adam was different. He was the only friendly person in a sea of others who went about their business as if she was invisible. Adam looked like Phil, too, with his blond hair and wide smile. *Mustn't think of Phil.* Adam might not have left yet. If she went back for the apple she could see him again. Just once more. Then she would drive home and forget him.

She parked neatly and returned to the entrance of the huge corporation where she asked the receptionist to let her in again. While walking up the stairs, Donna thought about Adam – the way he flicked his wrist to see his watch, the way Phil did. *Phil – was it only four weeks since he'd walked out?* She forced her thoughts back to Adam.

31

"Have you worked in investments before?" he asked last Monday morning. When she shook her head, intimidated by the hustle and bustle, and the sheer size of the floor with its hundreds of cubicles, he laughed kindly. "Feel free to pop in if you have any questions," he said. "My office is the middle one on the right over there. I'll be glad to help."

He had insisted on showing her how to access files using the special software, although more than once he'd confused her instead of helping her. She listened to him, but then did it her own way, which seemed to work out just fine. When Adam bent over her, his aftershave reminded her of Phil. *Oh, Phil, I do miss you.*

Donna blinked away tears. She reached the floor she wanted and opened the door to find that everyone was still working. Adam said they worked a half-day on Fridays. Why hadn't they gone home?

She closed the door behind her, glanced towards the desk that had been hers for a whole week, and spotted the apple near the monitor. She had to pass Adam's office on the way and decided to speak to him, but then a knot of people stopped right in front of her to argue over a computer printout. While she tried to find a way round them, Adam's phone rang, and his voice carried clearly through the open doorway.

"Adam here. ... Where's who? ... The temp? ... She's left. Must've had enough of us."

Donna gasped. Was he talking about her? He'd **told** her to go. Said everyone would be leaving because it was Friday. There must be some mistake. She went to knock on his door, but stood – hand raised – on hearing what came next.

"She's not good enough, Charles. God-awful dim. I had to show her a dozen times how to use StokTrak. And she never shut down. Anyone could've seen what she was working on."

Donna didn't know what hurt more – her pride or her heart. She felt completely betrayed. If Charles had been thinking of employing her, he sure as hell wouldn't now! She should never have come back for the apple.

She fled to her desk. Angry and upset, she grabbed the apple and slammed it so hard into the bin that it stuck in the wire mesh. Her head niggled with pain and she knew that if she didn't take something quickly, she would be suffering a full-blown migraine. *Damn Adam! Damn, damn, damn him! Whatever made her think he was like Phil?*

She washed down a tablet with gulps of water from her sports bottle, and sat down while trying to control her emotions. Then she noticed a confidential inter-office envelope in her tray. It hadn't been there when she left. It was from Charles Bristow and was addressed to her. She could feel something small and oblong inside – probably a dictation tape.

Work for next week? Perhaps. But Adam had just told Charles she'd gone home, so he would give this to someone else. Anger rose again and she clenched her fists. *Not if she could help it!*

She took off her coat and marched to Charles Bristow's office, envelope in hand. He looked up and seemed surprised to see her when she tapped on his open door.

"Come in, Mrs. Evans. Shut the door, lass. I thought you'd gone home."

"I nearly did, but I came back and saw this in my tray and... and I wanted to ask if you need me next week. I can change my assignment if you do."

She tailed off. That was a lie. She didn't have an assignment yet.

Charles reached for the envelope and turned it over. "You didn't open it?"

"W-well, no. I heard Adam tell you I'd gone and thought you would give it to someone else. But I can come back next week."

She felt spots of color burning her cheeks, and she winced when familiar needles pierced her head. Charles eyed her with concern, and then gestured to a chair in front of his desk.

"Sit down, lass. I'm in the middle of something here. Can you wait while I finish?"

Donna was grateful for the chance to regain her composure. She took deep breaths to calm herself, and slowly relaxed. The pain in her head became a dull throb, and gradually eased. She watched Charles tap nimbly on his keyboard. He was a fat, plain man, with dark, oily hair that hung over his black, thick-rimmed glasses. She wondered how he'd won the heart of the attractive woman who smiled from a silver-framed photograph on his desk. In another frame, two small boys, dark-haired like their father, shared a swing and grinned happily.

She thought back to her own childhood, to the many times her parents had shouted at her to quit whining, and of the day she'd fallen off a swing and broken her arm. It had been bedtime before her mother realised she really was in pain. From then on, she'd kept her hurts and pains to herself, even after she'd married Phil. The headaches started a year ago, but she hadn't been to see a doctor. Too scared that she might have a tumor and that she would die suddenly, the way her mother had.

Phil had known something was wrong. "For God's sake, tell me. I'm not a bloody mind reader," he'd pleaded. But she'd bitten her lip and turned away from him when her head hurt. He'd accused her of not loving him, that she wanted someone else. That was probably why he'd left her and Vicky and gone to live with his mother.

A cough from Charles jolted her back to the present. He had picked up the envelope and was idly tapping the desk with it.

"Right, lass," he said in his thick, north of England accent. "Had a bit of a run in with our Adam, have ye? What d'you think of him?"

Donna wanted to shout '*He's a lying, two-faced, son of a bitch!*' Instead she hesitated.

"He seemed to be trying to help," she said, finally.

"The last temp called him a pain in the rear, interrupting her all the time and poking round her desk. He said you never turned your computer off. Did you?"

"No, I didn't, because he said he had rights to some of the files. But no-one could have accessed your folder. I changed the password every day."

Charles thrust the envelope at her. "Open it," he said.

She unwound the red twine and tilted the much-used inter-office envelope. While pulling out two sheets of paper, a miniature chocolate bar fell onto Charles' desk. He picked it up and handed it back to her.

"A little token of my appreciation," he said.

Donna's eyes lit up with pleasure when she read the documents. Her heart pounded with joy when she recognised them as being a formal offer of employment.

"What d'you say, lass?"

"Oh, yes, yes please. Thank you very much."

"Before you get too carried away, you should know that it won't just be me you'll be reporting to. You'll be working for Adam, too, and he's got his own candidate for the job. He'll do his best to trip you up. It could be nasty."

She tilted her head defiantly. "I can handle him."

Charles beamed. "Right, just sign on the dotted line. Both copies. The bottom one's yours."

While Donna signed her name with a flourish, Charles came round his desk and held out his hand for the top copy.

"Go straight to Personnel on Monday," he said. "They'll work out a fee with the agency tonight. Welcome aboard."

He held out a podgy hand. Donna shook it and, with her feet hardly touching the ground, waltzed back to her desk to retrieve her coat and bag. Some people were leaving their desks and there was no sign of Adam. So they did go home early on Fridays, but not **that** early.

As she made her way to the exit, she decided to call Phil to share her good news, but first she would tell him about her headaches. Then she would tell him how much Vicky missed her daddy, and how much she missed him, too.

On the landing outside the fourth floor, she started singing loudly. She danced down the marble stairs until she arrived at the next landing where she was momentarily disconcerted to see Adam and a trim, blonde girl looking at her in surprise. Her first instinct was to ignore them, to treat Adam with the contempt he deserved, but – wait a minute. Hadn't she just boasted she could handle him?

She smiled demurely and wished them a good weekend. A few steps down the next flight of stairs, however, she couldn't resist calling up at them, "See you on Monday!"

It had been worth coming back for the apple.

****

And here's another story about life in the office. This one is (to the best of my recollection) true. It took place fifty years ago, before personal computers came on the scene. Most typists still used manual typewriters, although electric ones were coming on the scene, and copy documents were produced by interleaving carbons between sheets of paper. To make multiple copies, typists cut stencils, wound them round a heavily-inked drum on a Gestetner or Roneo, and turned the machine's handle while counting out the required number. There was no handing the job over to a Xerox machine and letting it perform automatically in those days.

****

FOLLOWING A LEGEND

Olive Collier (or Olly Colly as she was always known) had a fearsome reputation. She had been secretary to the Agriculturist for twelve years, had an immense capacity for work, and ran the office like a drill sergeant. Everything – from rain gauges to hoarded reams of foolscap paper – occupied neatly labeled places in her huge supplies cupboard. Nobody walked in her office in muddy boots or failed to send in weekly reports.

But then Olly Colly moved into Accounting and I, fifteen years her junior, stepped into her legendary shoes. I worked very hard, and gradually people stopped comparing me with the Agriculturist's old secretary, and Olly's reputation no longer intimidated me.

Everything went smoothly until I had to update the Fieldstaff Reference Book, measuring 6½ in. by 8 in, while my boss was on holiday. It had been years since the book had been revised and some sections needed to be completely retyped. However, given no setbacks, I believed I could finish the job in ten days.

Bright and early on Monday morning, I cleaned the keys of my faithful Remington, and looked for a box of stencils. The reference book had been mimeographed and I wanted to keep its appearance consistent, so off I went to the Print Room, only to find that the

Gestetner duplicator had been disposed of, and all copying was being done on an offset-litho machine. Thanking my lucky stars that I hadn't started cutting stencils, I skipped back to my office and began hammering out originals on plain A4 paper.

I'd typed several sheets when it dawned on me that my pages were wider and longer than those in the reference book. Heck! Why hadn't I thought of that before? I rummaged through the supplies cupboard but found nothing remotely near 6½ in. by 8 in. A call to the Print Room produced an unhelpful "You must be joking! We only stock A4 and A3 so if you want anything else, you'll have to get it yourself." Frustration built up. With my boss on holiday I had the chance to catch up on lots of neglected tasks, but first I had to get the reference book out of the way.

The offending manual lay open in front of me, and I examined it closely. The sheets stacked neatly on top of each other and the text was flawlessly typed. Well, I could type as accurately as Olly Colly, but what paper had she used? My hand hovered over the phone, but pride got the better of me. I'd be *hanged* if I would ask Olly Colly what she used! Anyway, the Print Room only stocked A4, so A4 it would have to be.

I started typing again, this time leaving wide margins on the left and at the bottom so that, after guillotining the pages, I would end up with uncut edges at the top and on the right. The reference book should still look presentable.

Later, when the new girl in the Print Room proudly delivered fifteen sets of thirty sheets, I was stunned to find that she had centered every sheet. I told her to do the job again.

"But nobody leaves margins like that," she wailed, tears welling in her young eyes. "Please don't make me do it again. I'll get the sack if I waste that much paper."

I remembered my first job – how mortified I'd been when I made mistakes.

"I'll see what I can do," I promised.

In my haste, I didn't stop to think about the best way to do the job. After feeding a thick wad into the manual guillotine, I chopped the same width of both sides. On each cut, the pile of paper fanned under the blade, resulting in some margins being nearly half-an-inch wider at the bottom than at the top. Also I should have made the left margin wider to accommodate the ring holes. I tossed the ruined sheets away and cradled my head in my hands.

The phone rang and I reached to answer it. While speaking, I opened the reference book in the middle and idly pushed the stacks of pages together so that they met under the rings.

Bingo! I saw the light!

Olly Colly had used foolscap paper which she then cut precisely in half. I didn't know whether to laugh or cry – to laugh at myself for being so slow on the uptake, or to cry because of all the time and paper I'd wasted. A short call to Olly Colly would have prevented all that.

A week later, I asked the fieldstaff to bring in their reference books and duly updated each one. I was glad the job was over, but I took to heart the lessons I had learned while struggling with it. My first resolution was to plan a job before leaping into action, and the second (more important than the first) was to acknowledge that I didn't know everything and that I should seek advice when stumped – even if it meant going humbly to that fount of all knowledge, Olly Colly herself.

****

Here's a bit of trivia for you. One of our games at family gatherings was to make up titles of books. I bet you played that, too. Here are a few of my contributions:

WHAT'S ON YOUR SHELF?

The Final Goodbye	Millicent Flowers
Nobody Believes Me	Hugh Wood
Middle East Recipes	Allah Khat
Crossing the Desert	Mustapha Kamel
Mother's Advice	Maria Richman
She's On A Roll	Willie Enditt
Providing an Alibi	Justin Case
Scratch My Back	Godiva Baddich
Another Chance Lost	Misty Dedlyne
Nothing to Worry About	X Septimus Paye
The First Female Admiral	Piper Abbord
Dodging the Law	Ivan Allabye
Feeling Queazy	Henrietta Noista
Going on a Dream Holiday	Farrah Way
Changes Ahead	Watt Sapnin
Will There Be Rain?	May B. Layter

****

I had to try a new genre in my next writing assignment, i.e., fantasy. I'm too old and set in my ways to believe in fairies, witches, magic, werewolves and vampires. However, I gave it a go.

Here's what I wrote, and I'm happy to say that my tutor loved it!

****

TELLING TAILS

When the witch's spell started to work – the morning after Cindi's crazy party – it hurt like hell. Jason's skin split at his coccyx and something slid out. Slimy. No, wormy. No, worse than wormy. More like snake. Cold, thin, hard, it reached up into the small of his back.

It happened just after he'd lied to Mom about there being no booze or pills at the party. Okay, so there'd been some, but **he** hadn't had any. The hard, wiry thing snaked up another couple of inches. *What the hell was happening?*

He pulled down his shorts and twisted his backside towards his bedroom mirror.

Omigod! He had a tail!

And the tail had a mind of its own. It coiled itself into a ring, and then stretched out to tickle his buttocks, very delicately, with its slightly pink tip.

Jason yanked up his shorts and burst out of the room.

"You okay?" he heard his mother call when he dashed out of the front door.

"Sure!" he shouted back.

The tail zoomed up three more inches, nearly reaching his waist band.

Cindi. He had to get to Cindi. As he jogged the short distance to her place, he thought back to last night. It had been one hell of a party. Cindi had thrown it because her parents were away and she had the house to herself.

She had teased him into seeing the old hag crouched over a glass ball in a makeshift tent in the yard. Man, she was something that witch. Straight out of Wizard of Oz – hooked nose, bent chin, warts, beady black eyes, and long tangled hair. Even her skin looked green under the colored bulb dangling in the tent. He remembered the creepy way her cloak rustled when she bent forward and spread her crooked fingers towards the crystal ball. Her cackle was something else, too.

Jeez, the Wicked Witch of the West had nothing on her.

Cindi was in the front yard, a large trash bag at her feet, spilling empty beer cans and paper plates. She was handling a broken hydrangea with disgust, trying to lift its heavy bloom while avoiding the puke dripping from it. Somebody had crashed into the flower bed last night and thrown up. Jason hoped it wasn't him. Now wasn't a good time to wail about his tail. He grabbed a half-eaten stick of teriyaki from the litter, pushed off the meat, and looked around for string. Aha! That crushed party hat had a tassel. While Cindi held the bloom in place, Jason bound the stick to the plant's stem. The tassel was red and glaringly obvious, but it would do for now, he thought.

"Thanks, Jason." Cindi pushed her tousled hair out of her eyes with the back of a dirty hand. "Just look at this place! Gotta get it straight before Mom and Pop get home tonight."

"I must be psychic. I thought you'd need some help."

Cindi looked up at him sharply. Her eyes gleamed. "Is that why you came over?"

"Yeah. Of course."

The tail grew and did a u-turn. It tapped his hairy leg below the hem of his shorts.

Cindi eyed it and positively smirked. "No, it wasn't," she said.

Jason tried to push the tail back into his shorts but it kept avoiding his fingers. While Cindi laughed hysterically, Jason heard again the spiteful cackle of the old witch.

"You **knew** this would happen!" he shouted.

"No, I didn't."

A replica of Jason's tail shot out from below Cindi's armpit and wagged, like a warning finger, in front of her nose.

"Damn you," Cindi spluttered.

"Get hold of the witch," Jason urged. "Make her undo this."

"Can't. Dunno where she is, but from what she said at Levi's party, I guess I'm stuck with **this**," – Cindi pulled the tail out of her pants at waist level and swung it round like a jump rope – "for nearly a year. What did you do?"

"I had a can in my hand and she asked me if I was old enough to drink it. I said 'Course', then she muttered something like 'Tell the truth my jumped-up friend, or it will bite you in the end'. Didn't think she meant my **rear** end."

Jason rubbed his backside. The tail crept up and held his hand as if to comfort him.

"Can we go inside?" he begged. "Someone might see us out here."

"Gotta get this yard straight first."

As if understanding the situation, both tails slipped out of sight. Jason felt his wrap around his waist. He grabbed a trash bag out of the box and sped round the yard, collecting armfuls of empty cans and messy plates and stuffed them in the bag. Cindi concentrated on pulling gaudy play string off the shrubs. In twenty minutes, the yard was respectable again.

Cindi looked around and nodded her approval. "Now we can go indoors."

They dumped the trash and headed for the bathroom.

Cindi looked at herself with distaste. "I need a shower," she said, and bent to turn on the spray.

"Can I come in too?"

"As long as you keep your – everything to yourself."

They stripped off and lingered under the refreshing water. Their tails started playing peekaboo, before twining together at the tips.

"Pack it in!" Cindi commanded.

Jason's tail drooped despondently, and hung down his leg, but Cindi's wiggled onto his thigh. Jason slapped it.

"Ouch! That hurt."

"Sorry, Cindi."

They dried and wandered naked into the bedroom where they gazed morosely at their images in the mirror.

"Why is yours so long?" Jason asked. "You didn't go near the witch last night, and, anyway, who have you lied to? You've been on your own here."

Cindi pulled a face. "I've had mine a week."

"A week?"

"Yeah, since Levi's party last Friday. That was a gas, so I booked her for mine. Jeez, I wish I hadn't told her I was twenty-one. I didn't cotton on when she laughed and said 'That's a fine tale. Now **you'll** have one for twelve full moons'."

"D'you reckon anyone else got a tail, too?"

"Guess not. You're the only one who's come round today," Cindi glanced at him, "with your tail between your legs."

"What are we gonna do?"

"If you tell the truth, it shrinks a bit."

"You mean we gotta live with it? Make the best of it?"

"Make the **most** of it. Let me show you."

Cindi took Jason's hand and led him to the bed, where they sat on the edge.

"Do you like this?" she murmured, leaning against him and playing lightly with his chest hair.

Jason's tail crept round and grabbed Cindi's near her coccyx, and Cindi's did the same to his. They were bound together by a hard, tight ring which pulsed and tingled with Jason's sudden desire. He tried to speak, but only managed a low growl.

"Your tail tells me you do." Cindi snaked her arms around Jason's neck and her impudent nipples teased his chest. "But I want you to tell me."

Her eyelashes brushed his cheek, and she nuzzled closer.

"Just don't ..."

Her parted lips crept towards his.

"be ...

Jason crushed her to him.

"too honest."

****

Er, um, I'm still blushing. Let's get onto safer ground. And what could be safer than Scrabble? I love playing Scrabble, but don't get much chance these days. A couple of the matches I played delighted me so much I wrote stories about them. Here they both are. The first one is very short.

ANYMORE

The four of us in our clique at the Senior Center had a lively debate about words that writing software persistently made into one, the main victim being 'any more'. Paul, a retired English teacher, was vociferous in his condemnation of the practice, even though 'anymore' was listed in the Scrabble dictionary.

"I'll never use it," he declared.

We all laughed at him and opened up the Scrabble board. Paul apparently picked up good tiles, because he only changed one of them each time his turn came around.

It was a fast game and the bag emptied fast, until there was only one tile left in it, and it was Paul's turn. He drew out the tile – an R. He jiggled it in one hand while fingering his rack with the other. YEOMAN, that's what his other letters spelled. He put down the R at the end of his rack and discarded a B. If nobody used the Y at the beginning of Brenda's last word, YEAST, he could win by scoring on a triple with YEOMANRY – if Brenda's Y remained free.

Colin scored 36 on another triple at the top of the board. That left him with one tile, and Paul could tell – we could all tell by the way Colin had been looking for a free U – that he held the Q. However, he was ahead and could still win, even after deducting 10.

It was Dorothy's turn next, then Paul's. The game hinged on what she put down. She rearranged her tiles again and again, and a bead of sweat trickled down Paul's neck. The air prickled. Colin and Brenda looked at each other. They could see Paul was trying hard to stay nonchalant.

After shuffling her tiles one more time, Dorothy made SATYR, taking Paul's coveted Y. She had three tiles left.

Paul flopped in his chair. His arms drooped so that his fingertips touched the floor.

"Oh, I'm sorry," Dorothy said, looking at him with eyes that were too wide and innocent. "Did I spoil something for you?"

"Just a bit."

He moved the tiles around on his rack. Then, with a start, he realised he had a complete word. He could win the game, even without the extra 50. But it was a word he detested, a word he had vowed never to use.

"Come on, Paul," Brenda urged. "Put us out of our misery."

Paul shook his head, but then, reluctantly, put down ANYMORE to win the game.

****

THE LAST WORD

Carol sighed. One week to go to Christmas. There would only be her and Matt this year. No visitors, and Christmas just wasn't Christmas without visitors.

She'd sent cards and presents to friends and family. Their girls had responded with brightly-wrapped gifts that now lay under the tree, ready for Christmas morning, and, in keeping with an old tradition, she'd wrapped a small gift and placed it under the tree, too, just in case they had a visitor.

On Christmas Eve the skies over Wausaukee were burdened with snow and, in the weak daylight, the lake gleamed with cold, as if made of steel. When darkness fell, fluffy flakes of snow nestled in Carol's hair when she and Matt plodded carefully to their car after attending the evening service. 'Goodbyes' and 'Merry Christmases' echoed around the parking lot. Matt had parked their small sedan in the far corner, so he and Carol found themselves at the end of the line of cars that inched onto the main road.

"Brrum, brrum, brrrr, chucka, chucka---."

"Someone's in trouble," Carol said, peering back towards the church.

Matt swung the wheel and turned the car towards the sound of the dying engine. In the opposite corner, a man pushed open the driver's door of a pickup and jumped out. He lost his footing on the slippery surface.

Carol wound down her window and called, "Do you want a jump start?" Then she turned to Matt. "It's Ronnie. Look, hon, it's Ronnie."

"Hi, Carol." Ronnie slammed his door shut and crunched towards them. "Thanks, but I reckon this battery's had it. Guess I need a new one. Can you give me a ride to the gas station?"

The snow fell faster. Matt had the wipers going, but they barely cleared the windscreen. "No can do," he said. "The station's miles away. We need to get home. So do you."

Carol pulled her phone out of her pocket and offered it to Ronnie. "Can someone come and pick you up?"

Ronnie shook his head. Snowflakes clung to his eyelashes and hid the tartan of his warm jacket. "No. Nobody's home."

"Were you going to spend Christmas on your own?" Carol asked. "You can't do that. Come stay with us for a couple of days. We've got the room. And the turkey." She smiled up at him. "Please say yes."

Matt stuck an arm out of his window and jerked a thumb towards the back of the car. "Hop in, man," he said. "If we don't get started soon, I can see us getting stuck here. This is turning into a blizzard."

Ronnie climbed in and brushed off snow before blowing on his hands and rubbing his cold cheeks.

Matt closed his window and drove cautiously out of the parking lot. He leaned forward, squinting to see through the swirling flakes, coaxing the car through deepening drifts. The journey that had taken half an hour on Christmas Eve took three times as long and they didn't reach home until the small hours of Christmas Day.

In the privacy of their bedroom, with Ronnie already snoring in the spare room, Carol said a heartfelt thank you to God for bringing them safely home. "'Night, hon," she whispered to Matt. "Sleep tight, and Happy Christmas." He mumbled something and fell asleep. She lay on her back, watching the snow tumbling past the uncovered window until she too drifted into sleep's warm embrace.

It was ten o'clock on Christmas morning before Ronnie came into the kitchen where his hosts were enjoying coffee and croissants.

"Morning, all. Umm, something smells good."

"Help yourself, man. I'll dig out a disposable razor for you. Then I'll start making dinner." Matt grinned. "That's my present to Carol. She gets to do nothing today, except eat and sleep. And she doesn't have to sleep if she doesn't want to."

"Sleep? On Christmas Day? Well, I guess I might have a nap after dinner."

"What are you going to do until then?" Ronnie asked.

"I'll go for a stroll in the woods if I can find my boots. Get some fresh air in my lungs."

Matt laughed. "You'll have to shovel your way out first. We're snowed in."

"Well, then, I'll help you get dinner."

"You might change your mind if we open our presents," Matt said.

"Oo, what have you got for me?"

"Something you've wanted for a long time. Shall we open them now?"

"Why not? Hey, hey, I love Christmas. Bring your coffee over here, Ronnie. There's a little something under the tree for you, too."

"For me? But how...?"

"I've got second sight. Didn't you know?"

--o--

Carol left the presents from the girls under the tree and handed Ronnie his gift. He was very pleased with the pocket diary and the $10 gift card. Matt was delighted with "What's *Cooking in Wisconsin*" from Carol, and she was thrilled with his gift – a high-quality game of Scrabble – a replacement for the dilapidated board that they had played with for so long.

"Can we have a game now? Just one?" Carol pleaded.

"Told you!" Matt winked at Ronnie, who was gulping the last of his coffee.

"Give me a minute to freshen up, Carol, and I'll play you," Ronnie offered.

"You're on!"

Matt handed a packet of razors to Ronnie and pointed out the bathroom. "You don't know what you're letting yourself in for," he said. "Carol loves Scrabble. She won't let you get away with just one game."

Ronnie laughed. "Okay by me," he said. "Let's have a best-of-three."

--o--

Carol won the first game by a narrow margin but Ronnie coasted to victory in the second after he placed QUETZAL on a triple, joining the T and the L onto other words.

"Even Stevens," Carol said. They tipped the tiles back in the bag. "Next one is the decider."

"To be continued," Matt said. "Dinner's ready."

--o--

Two hours later, with the dishwasher chugging in the kitchen, Carol and Ronnie sat on either side of the small table they'd used in the morning and set the Scrabble board up again.

"Ladies draw first," Ronnie said.

Carol smiled and dipped her hand in the bag. She drew out a G. Ronnie drew an E. They threw those tiles back in the bag, shook it, and selected seven tiles each.

Ronnie started. He swapped his tiles around a few times, and then laid TRIBAL, placing the T on the blue double.

"Eighteen to Ron," said Matt, who was keeping score.

Carol jiggled her tiles, then laid ANGRILY on the board, placing the A under Ronnie's L.

"Nice, hon. That gives you a total of 65."

Ronnie pointed to the board. "Can she have LA?"

"Sure she can. It's the first word in the Ls. It's the sixth tone in the diatonic musical scale."

"Okay, but you're gonna be sorry, missus."

"Oh, oh. I've let you in on that triple, haven't I? Do your worst."

Starting with the double, four squares down from the top right of the board, Ronnie slowly laid Q – U – E – A – Z – Y, the Y being at the end of ANGRILY. "Howzat!"

Matt laughed. "One hundred and eleven to Ron, making him 129. You've got some catching up to do, hon."

Carol's next move only scored six. She added SOD in front of the A in QUEAZY.

"That brings you to 71, hon."

"Thank you, Carol. I'll take that nice double." Ronnie added SHRINK to the S of SODA.

"Thirty more to Ron. Total: 159."

"I can catch up a bit here," Carol said, "and I only need three tiles." Using the N in SHRINKS, she made JINX.

"Thirty-six, hon. This is quite a game. Between you, you've used the four highest-scoring tiles in six moves. Your turn, Ron."

"Let's open it up a bit." Ron placed ENVY on the board, the Y going under LA.

"ENVY and LAY give you eighteen. Total of 177."

"I'm staying up here." Carol used the H in SHRINKS to make WHOLE.

"Not bad, hon. That 22 makes your total 129."

Ronnie grinned. "I hoped you'd do that. Now I can really open it up." He added five more tiles under the V in ENVY to make VELVET.

"Nice play, man. VELVET earns you 39 on the triple and brings your total to 211. What are you going to do, hon?"

"I'll match it!" Carol gleefully laid all seven tiles, starting with the T of VELVET to start TAPIOCAS. which ended on the right hand bottom triple. "Hee, hee," she giggled. "That's twice I've got all my tiles out."

"Good play, hon. You score 39 on the triple, plus 50 for using all your tiles. Total is 218."

Ron rubbed his chin. "I'm going to have to use my blank. It's a V." He added a W, two Es, an I and the blank to join up with the L in VELVET, making WEEVIL.

"Sixteen to Ron. Total now 232."

"I'll take that!" Carol made POET, placing the E and T under Ron's W and E.

"POET, WE and ET score 24. You're ten in the lead, hon."

"Not for long. I'll use my other blank as an S to make GRIPES, with your P in POET it gives me a triple." Ron dug in the bag and pulled a face when he saw his new tiles. "Aaagh. Your turn, Carol."

"I've got choices," she said, "but I'll lay MINDER, ending on the R in TRIBAL. What does that give me?"

"Eighteen. It brings you one ahead of Ron. This is going to be really close."

Carol crossed her fingers, expecting Ronnie to take advantage of the isolated letters in MINDER, but he didn't seem to be interested in that part of the board.

"Thank you, Carol," he said. "Now I can get rid of all these Os." He placed two Os after the middle V of VELVET, added a D, then two more Os.

"VOODOO, eh? On a double. Nice, Ron. You're back in the lead. Total is 277."

"It's my turn to say not for long. I can beat that." Carol put down four tiles to create FAMED, availing herself of the M in MINDER.

"You earned 26 on the double, hon. Total, 286. Your turn, Ron."

Ronnie used the D of MINDER to form TREND.

"Eight, seeing the R is worth three. Total – 285. It's neck and neck again."

Carol pulled a face. "There aren't many good tiles left. I can make GAUNT, ending on the T in TREND. Does that put me back in the lead?"

"Yup, by eight, but Ron's still got plenty of tiles."

Ron swapped his tiles back and forth on the rack. "I have a four-letter word, but it won't fit in anywhere. And even if it could, it'll only give me seven. I can score that just using one tile."

He reached to the top of the board and laid an A in front of the S of SHRINKS.

"As you say, AS and AW give you seven. Total of 292. You're one behind again, man."

"I don't believe it! I don't believe it." Carol bounced on her chair like a five-year-old. "I've won. I've won."

Slowly and deliberately, working from right to left and starting before the A of AS she laid an M, then a T, an S, an I, an R, an H, and finished with a C. "CHRISTMAS. Howzat?" she cried.

"Congratulations, hon. What are you left with, Ron?"

"A, B, F, T and two Us."

"Right. You lose eleven points and end with 281. Carol gains those eleven, plus 57 for the top triple, plus 50 for using all her tiles, so her total score is 411. She wins by 130."

Carol clapped her hands. "I couldn't believe my eyes when you put down that A so I could make CHRISTMAS. What a word to end the game with, eh?"

"It's definitely, positively, absolutely the best word you could lay," Ronnie agreed. "Here's wishing you both and everyone else a very happy Christmas."

54

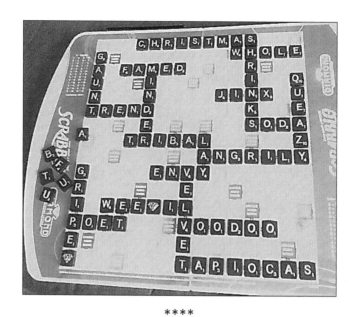

****

The first piece of writing that LongRidge asked for was a memoire – something that would tell them more about me – so I wrote about being evacuated from my London home at the start of World War II. Those were dismal days at first, and I described them with reluctance, but they got happier as time went on. The following stories describe three periods of my life, all very different from each other.

****

A PLACE OF SAFETY

Memories are like seed pearls trapped in a dim recess of our psyche. Each recall of the moment can bring with it pleasure, laughter, satisfaction, pride, fear, or such shame that we squirm at the memory decades later. I like to think of that recess as a small, velvet-lined box. Occasionally I poke a mental finger into it and roll the pearly memories around, lingering on the cherished ones, like the births of my children, but I rarely touch the seed pearls of my childhood, stuck as they are in the corners, and it is with hesitation that I stir them now.

My mother would blame it all on the war. I was three when World War II broke out and my father, who was in the Reserves, was recalled to active duty.

Before September 1939, we were a happy, typically poor family. Dad hadn't planned to marry. He enjoyed his life as a soldier in the Royal Signals and expected to stay in the Army, but, after a brief dalliance when he and my mother were stationed at the same Army barracks in Aldershot, Mum found she was in the family way – the usual term for being pregnant in those days. Dad had been raised to 'do the right thing' (another old expression) and they got married, even though there was a good chance that the coming baby was not his. "You make your bed and you lie in it," he used to say, and he practised what he preached.

We moved around a lot between 1935 and 1939. Bessie, the cause of the marriage, was born when our parents lived in

Dagenham with our grandparents. Shortly afterwards, we moved to Hornchurch, not that far away, where Lily and I were born. Then we went back to Dagenham where Tony arrived. We lived in rooms or flats rented from the local council, none of which had a garden, but we three little girls played in the street like other kids.

Dad had enlisted in the Royal Signals branch of the British Army when he was eighteen, and served in India and Malaya before going into the Reserves in 1934. He was a general labourer when Bessie was born, but had become a panel beater by the time we moved to Hornchurch. There he worked for Briggs Motor Bodies, later famously known as Fords of Dagenham. In September, 1936, just after I was born, he was mobilized at Aldershot and was posted to 'A' Corps of the Royal Signals, and transferred to Army Reserves, Section B, in November, 1936. He then became a postman until recalled to active duty in August, 1939, three weeks after the birth of Tony, his cherished only son. He was stationed in Harpenden, in Essex, which meant he would get leave – not often – but he would be able to see his family now and again.

England and France declared war on Germany on 3rd September, 1939, and Mum and we four children were evacuated to Woodbridge in Suffolk. Nearly one and a half million children were evacuated from the London area. Most evacuees travelled by train to rural districts of England and Wales. However, our family went by paddle steamer.

The London Evening News reported in September, 1939, that: "Of all the evacuation schemes, none was more striking than that by which nearly 11,000 Dagenham schoolchildren, teachers, helpers and mothers, were taken by water from the Ford Works Jetty at Dagenham to Yarmouth, Lowestoft, and Felixstowe. The whole scheme was first thought of only last Monday, and the Ford Works and the General Steam Navigation Company co-operated with the local authorities, eight of the company's famous pleasure steamers being lent for the job."

So it was that, Mum (with Tony in her arms), Bessie (four), Lily (nearly two) and I (just turned three) walked from Beverley Road to the Ford Works Jetty very early on the morning of 3rd September, 1939 – the day war was officially declared. A neighbour helped Mum with her hold-all, and we all carried bundles, labels flapping on our lapels, gas masks over our shoulders.

Mum later described the evacuation for me. She wrote:

"A woman visited the homes and left a list of what could and could not be taken. One change of clothes for babies, change of underclothes for others. Milk for baby. No other food.

I woke you about 4 a.m. as we had to be at Dagenham Docks about 5. I had Bess, you, Lily and Tony (under 2 months old), plus a hold-all and handbag. A neighbour, with two of her own children, helped me. We walked to Dagenham Docks from Beverley Road, and we were on board early. It was a biggish boat. We didn't know where we were going until we were outside the 3-mile limit. There were no seats and we had to make do as best we could on the cold deck. The boat docked at Felixstowe, and we were transferred to coaches that went to Woodbridge. We had been given soup on the boat. It was a relief to sit down on a proper seat in the coach."

Mum didn't say which paddle steamer we boarded, but, according to the *London Evening News*, it would have been either the *Crested Eagle*, *Medway Queen*, or the *Thames Queen*.

The first night at Woodbridge was chaotic. We were crammed into a barn and slept on straw. Local people brought milk for the children, bless their hearts. Two days later, Mum was allocated an empty house in Edwin Avenue. Her neighbour, Mrs. Peacock, was very helpful. *"Not"*, as Mum wrote, *"like lots of others who didn't like the evacuees."* Our house had a seven-foot wall built a few feet in front of it as protection from bomb blasts.

We were very lucky. Our house had two bedrooms and a long back garden, and it was so near to the shops that, little as we were, we could walk there. We were hard-up, of course, as was everyone else. Dad's pay went straight to Mum, I believe, but it was never enough and we often had potato crisps and a cup of Oxo for dinner. You could buy four Oxo cubes for a penny in those days.

I don't know what got into Mum after a while. Either she couldn't cope, or maybe she just hated being in the country. She made friends with people whom Dad described as "doubtful" and let the house fall into such a dreadful state that we lived in squalor. It got so bad that the police called in the NSPCC, but they took no action against Mum because she was pregnant with June, who wasn't Dad's baby.

During the difficult subsequent birth, Mum nearly died. Dad was allowed home on compassionate leave, and the doctor advised him to apply for an extension, which he did. He was disgusted by the state of the house. He burned every bit of bedding, scrubbed all the floors, cleaned the windows and washed down the paintwork. We four children had to go into isolation for a month at Bury St. Edmunds where we were daubed with gentian violet to combat our impetigo.

--o--

After that, Dad contacted the local branch of Dr. Barnardo's. He wanted to keep us together and was relieved when Mrs. Sheldrake, a widow, who had two grown daughters living with her, offered to take us in. There were not many people who would take on such a responsibility, especially at her age. She lived in New Street, Woodbridge, not far from Edwin Avenue, so Bessie could go to the same school, and I would join her there as soon as I was five. It seemed an ideal solution. In the first photo below, from left to right: Bessie, Dolly, Lily, Tony. Photos of 20 New Street follow it.

The photos of 20 New Street were taken in the 1990s, but when we lived there, Mrs. Sheldrake's house had a tiny garden in front of it, with a black metal gate, similar to the house next-door in the middle photo. Do you see that window in the roof in the last photo? That was our bedroom. We trudged up a steep narrow staircase to reach it.

Everything started well, but then Mrs. Sheldrake isolated us girls from family life. She adored Tony. He ate and slept in his own special place with either her or one of her daughters, but Bess, Lily and I were banished to a far different world.

We were not neglected the way Mum neglected us. We had regular meals and were kept clean and tidy. However, apart from attending school (daily and on Sunday), we spent our days in the chilly back scullery which had a brick floor and a small window that never opened. We sat on chopping blocks or on the cast iron base of an old mangle, underneath its worn, wooden rollers.

Life was particularly hard for Lily. For most of the time we were there, she was too young to go to school and spent day after day in that gloomy, spider-ridden place on her own, amusing herself as best she could with pencil and paper.

I'm afraid I wet the bed quite often and, for punishment, had to sleep on the bedroom floor under the wash table for a week. The table stood next to the eaves (our bedroom was in the attic) where mice squeaked as they scurried back and forth through holes in the skirting board. I dreaded those dark, scary nights when every rustle of the peeling wallpaper made me freeze, expecting little claws to run over me, or catch in my hair.

In 1943, with the escalation of hostilities, Dad expected to be posted to France at any time, and he came to see us. Poor Dad. He was shocked at what he found. Tony was fine, but Lily was a pale, painfully thin, nervous child. Bess and I were pale and skinny, too, and very, very wary. Mrs. Sheldrake laid tea in the front parlour – a room we only went through when we left the house – and there was cake! Lily burst into tears when asked if she would like another slice. We never had cake. Dad tactfully suggested to Mrs. Sheldrake that looking after the four of us was too much for her. She agreed, and Dad set about finding us another home.

--o--

He applied to the National Children's Home and Orphanage, first to their Harpenden Branch, but they had no vacancies. He then wrote to their Bramhope Branch near Leeds, in the West Riding of Yorkshire. They said they could take Bess, Lily and me, but not Tony because he was too young (not yet five), so our brother went to live with an aunt and uncle and their two boys, where he was very happy.

Talk about red tape!

I have all the letters that Dad wrote to the NCH&O. There were many forms he had to fill in three times over, because each child had to have her own set. We all needed combinations, liberty bodices, tunics and hair brushes. Then there were the ration books, clothing coupons and children's allowances to be dealt with. But Dad settled everything in six weeks.

We arrived at Bramhope on the 19th August, 1943, the day before my seventh birthday. I don't remember making the journey, but it must have been by train to Leeds, and from there by bus to the stop nearest to the Home. Dad was allowed to stay the night before he had to return to Dover Castle where No.8 Special Wireless Section of the Royal Signals was stationed.

There were ten houses in the Home; four for girls and six for boys. Butterfield II House, our home for the next four years, was a stone-faced building, a mirror-image of Butterfield I House. In the photo on the next page, Butterfield I is on the left-hand side. A door in our big dormitory (where fifteen girls slept) led into Butterfield I. Our identity numbers had to be marked on every piece of clothing, including hankies that we made out of the soft areas of old sheets. "Butterfield II" was shortened to "X2". Lily became X2.3, I was X2.9, and Bess was X2.23. Nowadays, I often use variations of my number for computer passwords.

I was happy at Bramhope, even though I once ran away with my best friend who wanted to go back to London. Bess didn't mind being there, but Lily hated it. Dad came to see us whenever he could, and so did Mum, after Dad gave her permission. He had been given custody of us after he divorced Mum when the war ended.

We followed an unvarying routine which wasn't onerous by any means. We were given jobs which increased in difficulty as we grew older. Little ones laid tables, scrubbed the benches in the boot and cloak rooms, or cleaned the taps on the circular marble fountain around which we gathered to wash our faces or clean our teeth. Nine- and ten-year-olds peeled buckets of potatoes, swept and polished rooms, and washed up after meals. The oldest girls cooked meals and lit fires. They had to leave the Home when they reached eighteen and find a job to support themselves.

Christmas was a special time. Father Christmas would arrive with a sack over his shoulder at about eight o'clock on Christmas Eve. He visited Butterfield I House first, and then came through the connecting door into our big dormitory, where he distributed small stockings before making his way to the other dormitory. We were allowed to play with the toys before settling down to sleep. The contents were always the same; discs on elastic that we made twirl and spin, miniature books, or puzzles and word games, a set of five-stones or a wooden top. The Friends of the Home gave these small presents to every child every year.

In the morning we would stand outside the Sisters' bedrooms and sing a carol before we dashed downstairs to find our big stockings. The evening before we'd each been given a real stocking (again provided by the Friends of the Home) which we labeled and placed in chosen spots in the wooden-paneled entrance hall. In the morning, we found they'd all been switched and we had to hunt for the right one. These stockings also contained small toys, usually knitted teddy bears or golliwogs (there was nothing incorrect about their name in those days), more books and puzzles, and maybe an apple.

After breakfast we walked in a long crocodile down to the beautiful Methodist Chapel in Bramhope to attend morning service. While we were gone, the older girls prepared Christmas dinner. After that was cleared away, the Sisters opened the "Post Office". Most of us were evacuees, and parents and friends sent presents to the Home. It often meant that the wealthier parents sent more than one gift, while true orphans or some evacuees would have received nothing had it not been for the Friends of the Home. Here again their generosity came into play for they ensured that no child was disappointed.

War was remote for us in Bramhope. We were forbidden to go to certain areas for fear of unexploded bombs but, during the four years I was there, I only heard air raid sirens a couple of times. The Avro Works at Bradford was a target for enemy bombers, as were the foundries in Sheffield. They weren't that far away. However, the enemy left us pretty much alone.

Finally the war was over and Dad was demobbed while holding the rank of Company Quarter Master Sergeant. In his release book, his commanding officer reported that his conduct had been exemplary throughout, and gave the following testimonial:

"I have known SQMS Piper for a number of years, the first two of which he served in my unit. During that time he has shown a great capacity for initiative, organization and hard work, and was awarded the British Empire Medal for sterling work in Normandy. A good leader of men, a good mixer socially, and always cheerful,

Piper is a man of the highest integrity, and I have no hesitation in recommending him."

After being demobbed, Dad was allocated a council house in Wembley and we left the Home. He had been re-employed by the Post Office and held an executive job in London, which meant we children spent long periods of time unsupervised, and he was criticized by the authorities for that.

A hardworking war widow worked in his office. She had a lively daughter, Pat, one year younger than Lily. Dad was impressed by how hard Mary worked, in spite of her chronic rheumatoid-arthritis and they entered into a marriage of convenience. We became a happy family. Events were against us, though, and – due to an interfering Catholic priest – the marriage didn't work out. However, as they say, that is another story.

****

Our new step-mother had a brother, Henry, married to Marie, a sweet-natured lady. They lived in Juniper Street, Stepney, and Aunt Marie sometimes gave us large tin boxes of broken biscuits that she was able to buy from a local public house: she didn't even have to return the boxes. One of those boxes came in really handy one weekend, as you will see in the next short memoire.

THAT TAKES THE BISCUIT – AND THE SUNDAY ROAST

In 1948, Wembley hosted the Olympic Games. I was twelve-years-old then. Flower baskets brightened gloomy Wembley Central station. Athletes lodged with local families, and some of their equipment was stored in a prefabricated hut erected in our school playground. Our Gym teacher, Bertha Crowther, competed in the Games. She came fifth in Heat 3 of the Women's 80-metre Hurdles, and sixth in the Women's High Jump.

Food was on ration, and we had few extras, so we really appreciated the boxes of broken biscuits that Aunt Marie gave us now and again. Aunt Marie had worked in Meredith & Drew's factory in Shadwell before it was destroyed in the Blitz. She went to work in the local pub which still bought its biscuits from M&D's new facility at High Wycombe.

One weekend, we had no gas or electricity as a result of another miners' strike, and had no way of cooking the Sunday joint. However, my Dad was a Quarter-Master Sergeant when he was in the Army and nothing stumped him. He built a trench on the concrete patio outside the back door of our council house, and filled it with twigs and firewood. He had a good fire going in no time. Then he turned one of the M&D boxes on its side, put a rack inside it, and roasted the half-shoulder of lamb on that. He took this photo at the time.

It shows my step-mother bending over a steaming saucepan, testing the potatoes, watched by Sally Jarman and her husband. The Jarmans were friends of Mum's who'd come to visit us that weekend. The M&D tin oven is bottom left, resting on the bricks.

I thought you would be interested to learn a little of Meredith & Drew's history. They founded a factory in Shadwell, London, in 1830, and received their first Royal Warrant from Queen Victoria in 1894. By 1946, they were the largest biscuit manufacturers in Britain.

Grace's Guide showed advertisements of M&D's delicious products in their 1954 editions. The photos included Custard Creams, Shortcake, Currant Shortcake, Bourbons, Lincolns, Crax and Lemon Fingers. I loved the Bourbons. So did Dad, and he always got to go through the broken biscuits first, so there weren't many left by the time it was my turn. I usually settled for Wafers or Custard Creams. Lincolns were always the last to be eaten. Meredith & Drew were bought out by United Biscuits in, I think, 1967, half a century ago, but we can still buy biscuits bearing their name. And Bourbons are still my favourite.

****

I end these memoires with an astonishing story about an adopted man who found his birth family sixty-six years after he was born. It transpired that I'd played an important part in the reunion: it only happened because I'd written a book (*The Gift*), using my maiden name.

****

A FAMILY FOUND

I hardly know where to begin with Alan's story. It's so incredible. If any one of the many "ifs" hadn't come about, we wouldn't have known he existed.

It all started with an e-mail.

Alan's son, Andrew, sent the following e-mail to my son, Paul, in September 2009:

"Hello. My name is Andrew Priestley. I am hoping you can help me. I am trying to find relatives of my father. He was born in 1943 with the name of James William Piper in Lindrick Emergency Hospital to an Elizabeth Jane Piper who was at that time married to a Harvey James William Piper, who – by the records I have been able to find – fathered Dorothy J. Piper who was born in 1936 in Romford. During our search we have found only one person by the name of Dorothy J. Piper born in that year. That person seems to be your mother. They were also the parents of Lily F. Piper, Harvey A.E. Piper, and June Piper.

At this point I would appreciate any help that you may be able to provide. As you can imagine, my father is quite anxious to find any living members of his family as he was adopted shortly after birth in 1943. I appreciate that this may be unknown to you or in fact your mother. Again, I hope that this finds you well and that you are inclined to help with my search. I also hope your mother's book, "The Gift" is a great success. I am not sure what to say at this point, except that I really look forward to your reply either way."

This e-mail out of the blue raised many questions, like: how had Andrew found Paul? How did he find me, and not Lily or June? How did he know I'd written *The Gift*? After relaying the message to me, Paul posed some of my questions to Andrew, who replied:

"... We then researched children born to Harvey James William Piper and Elizabeth Jane Piper (nee Welsh). By doing so we found the birth records for Dorothy, Lily, Harvey and June. And my father, James. The dates matched, so we then started a search on Google using the children's names. We found out that Harvey passed away in 2004, and the only other name that showed in the Google search engine was Dorothy's when she had a short story published in a newspaper article in America.

The information that the newspaper printed about Dorothy said that she was born in England and moved over to the USA in 1995, and also that she had a book published when she was 71. Those dates tied in with the birth date of the Dorothy we had found. We then googled the information about her book which gave us a web link to Ubuntu where you (Paul) had quoted the same article about your mother's book in 2008! This is why we contacted you, taking the risk of sending you the e-mail, hoping there was some link between your mum's family and my dad, and, blow me down with a feather, THERE WAS!

Lindrick Emergency Hospital was a temporary maternity hospital set up during the 2nd World War. It is now a golf club literally just a few miles outside of Worksop, in the district of Anston and located south of Dinnington."

Andrew added later that his dad had been brought up in Sheffield and married Sandra in 1965. They moved to Ireland in 1975 and settled in Kilcoole, not far from Wicklow, in 1977.

The wires between England and Ireland burned hot for hours when June rang Alan and had a very long chat with him. Excitement increased when he made arrangements to meet Lily and June while attending a school reunion. These reunions happened every summer. Alan, Sandra, June and Lily had a lovely get-together and I planned to meet Alan when visiting England in 2012. However, just before my trip, Alan fell ill and was diagnosed with brain cancer. We were all very worried about him, but he was upbeat during my 3-day visit when I met him and Sandra, son Matthew, and daughter Julie who brought her three children to see me.

For a while, Alan went into remission. In April, 2014, Julie reported that her dad was doing well, but by Christmas of that year, Alan was in a wheelchair. He gave up his physiotherapy business, and was in and out of hospital, the last time being in April 2015 when he suffered a massive chest infection. The 19th April was his and Sandra's Golden Wedding anniversary, and she spent the day with him in hospital.

He passed away on 17th June, 2015, and we mourned the loss of a wonderful man. Sandra had borne the strain of looking after him, and it told on her health. Two years later, she joined Alan in heaven.

In less than a decade I had found a brother and lost him again. It's very, very sad. On the bright side, I still have Julie and her lovely family, Matthew and Andrew. And, to think I would never have known any of them if I hadn't been a writer.

****

Let's have a change from prose. Here are a few of my poems. *Powder Puff Petticoats* was published in *Dance Magazine* when *Come Dancing* was my favourite programme on BBC television. The four poems about animals were composed during the period when my grandchildren were little, and I wrote the verses to amuse them. *The Rolling Stone* won 1st prize in the 2004 SouthWest Writers Contest, and gained heartening criticism from the Judge who said he laughed out loud at the last line. Lastly, I wrote *Little Man* and *Energy from Sand* after I became fascinated by science-fiction.

POWDER PUFF PETTICOATS

The spotlight is dimmed. In its shadowy beam
Comes, gracefully stepping, the formation team.
Like zephyrs at play in the faint mist of morn,
Or fragile seed balls on the breeze lightly borne,
To strains of a melody, dreamy and slow,
The powder puff petticoats waft to and fro.

The tempo increases. With effortless grace,
The billowing, dainty, trimmed layers of lace –
Like roses unfolding when kissed by the sun –
Reach upwards to heaven until, one by one,
With shame at such flirting, they shyly drift down
And play peek-a-boo 'neath a shimmering gown.

LIBERATION

Why should I put up with it, day after day?
This isn't a marriage – just some place to stay.
If it weren't for the kids, I would leave him today.
I'm earning enough now to pay my own way.
And who needs him?

The fighting is over. I felt pretty bad
When both boys decided to stay with their Dad.
I bet it's not long 'til they're driving him mad
With quarrels and whines over what they once had.
Let him handle them.

Now both of the girls want a place of their own.
No thanks for the years I have scrimped all alone
To pay for school trips, trendy clothes, and the 'phone.
They've not helped at all, but I ought to have known.
Now it's up them.

At last I can do what *I* want to do,
Get my nose in a book, join an evening class, too.
I can soak in the bath, no-one yells for the loo,
And the house looks a picture with everything new.
I can please myself.

Sue's wedding was lovely, and my Tom was there.
He gave me a smile when he passed by my chair.
Perhaps, thinking back now, he really did care,
And I should've spoke up when things didn't seem fair.
The kids would've helped if we'd taught them to share.
Now the family's scattered – Heaven knows where.
It's being so lonely that's hardest to bear.
And no-one needs me.

MA BAIRN

Ma bletherin' bairn, will ye hush a wee whiley!
Pray cease askin' questions and runnin' aroond.
The minute a-laughing, the next ye're a greetin'.
Faith, laddie, ye're wearin' me intae the groond.

Will ye look at yer claes, all fresh on the mornin'.
Just where d'ye find all the mud ye've been in?
Come here when ye're bid, or I'll gie ye a skelpin'.
Pray stop all that splashin'. I'm soaked to the skin.

Ma bonnie wee bairn, in your cot safely sleepin',
Braw arms round yon teddy bear friend tightly curled.
Yer mither an' father fond vigil are keepin'.
Too soon must ye learn o' the cares o' the world.

My second son was born over two weeks late. The tax year ended on 5th April in 1960, so his birth fell outside the 1960 tax year which would have given us a rebate in child allowance. However, in March, I was eligible to claim an early refund on the PAYE (Pay as you earn) tax I had paid while employed. We were desperately hard up, so I wrote to the Inspector of Taxes, to ask if he could let me have the refund before the tax year ended. Here's my plea:

Dear Inspector of Taxes,
I write with a view
To see if there's anything that you can do
To speed up the refund to which I am due,
'Cos we're broke.

I've left my employment and in seven weeks
We'll be losing our sleep when our new baby shrieks.
My hubby's on four-days – it looks like for keeps.
Life's no joke.

I know I should wait, but we're in a tight spot
And the bills that we owe come to more than we've got.
Could you rush my refund? That would help **such** a lot.
Okey doke?

My poem landed on the desk of someone who must have known what it was like to be hard up, and who also had a sense of humour. Not only did he process the refund immediately but he sent the following reply:

I hope you are right in your estimate
And the happy event's in seven weeks and not eight.
If it runs a bit over and baby is late
I'm sorry to say there'll be no tax rebate.

FOX TROTTING

Now Freddie the Fox had holes in his socks.
Fredrika, his wife, couldn't mend them.
He rang up the store to order some more
Instructing them where they should send them.
The store said, "Oh, dear, we've run out we fear.
We haven't a sock in the store, sir.
We'll find out today what has caused the delay,
And tell them we must have some more, sir."

Then, round about four, came a knock on the door.
It was Mole with a large invitation.
"Can you come, say you will, to our dance on the hill?
We have booked the best group in the nation." (The Beatles)
Of course they said 'Yes', and they hurried to dress
But all of Fred's socks were in tatters.
He started to cuss, but his wife said, "Don't fuss.
I don't suppose, dear, that it matters."

The evening was fun. They twirled and they spun
And hopped, for their friends were insisting.
An hour or more they stayed on the floor
A-rocking, a-rolling and twisting.
"Now let's have some blues, so kick of your shoes
And smooch round the floor nice and steady,"
The Emcee suggested. A tune was requested.
"Ah, this is so nice," murmured Freddie.

Then Cat called, "Behold! Fred's toes must be cold."
His partner purred, "Isn't it shocking.
I vow and declare Fredrika can't care
Her husband has more hole than stocking."
Fredrika blushed red. "I'm off home," she said,
And ran from the floor looking harassed.
"Don't go, too," cried a friend, so Fred stayed to the end,
Not feeling the least bit embarrassed.

After dancing all night, by the moon's pearly light,
To their homes tired dancers went flitting.
When he crept up to bed a surprise greeted Fred,
For Fredrika sat busily knitting. (Socks for her hubby)
Next day, at the store, stretched a queue past the door.
"We need socks!" everyone was declaring.
Fred chuckled to see that now, only he,
Had no holes in the socks he was wearing.

BUNNY BILL AND SISTER LIL

Say, do you know where rabbits go when winter comes around?
They curl up small, into a ball, and slumber underground.

Now Bunny Bill and sister, Lil, woke up one winter's day.
"Come back to bed," their mother said. "It isn't time to play."

She twitched her nose and rubbed her toes, then fell asleep once more.
"I'm bored," said Bill. "Me, too," said Lil. "Let's go out and explore."

So from their hole the bunnies stole. They both felt brave and bold,
And all around deep snow they found. They shivered in the cold.

They heard a noise. Some little boys threw snowballs with delight
'Til one said, "Gee, it's time for tea, and Santa comes tonight."

They stopped their play and ran away. The light began to fade.
"I'm scared," said Lil. "What for?" asked Bill. "You needn't be afraid."

The moon rose high up in the sky. Stars twinkled clear and bright.
"Look there!" cried Lil. Atop a hill a chapel blazed with light.

The church bells rang. The choir sang, "A babe lies in a stall.
God's only Son, the promised One, has come to save us all."

Both Bill and Lil sat very still and listened, 'til Bill said,
"We'd better go. It's late, you know. We ought to be in bed."

Soon, safe and sound, snug underground, Lil said, "We should tell Mum
Where we have been and what we've seen. I bet she'll wish she'd come."

"Of course we will," said sleepy Bill. "We'll tell her in the Spring."
But neither spoke when they awoke. They'd forgotten everything.

WILBERFORCE, THE WHALE

Come, listen, little children, while I tell you all a tale
Of a place called Bognor Regis, and of Wilberforce, the Whale.
He was very fond of doughnuts. There weren't any in the sea
So he swam to Bognor Regis, just to buy some for his tea.

When the vendor asked "How many?", "I will have them all," Will cried.
"They smell lovely, and I'm hungry. I missed lunch to catch the tide."
But the trippers who were waiting very quickly made a fuss.
"Well, he might have been more thoughtful and have saved a few for us."

Wilberforce was brought up nicely, and could see it wasn't fair,
So he passed the bag politely round the people who were there.
They each took one, and thanked him, and went back to sand and sea,
Then the Whale found, broken-hearted, "There is nothing left for me."

But the friendly doughnut-maker, seeing Wilberforce so sad,
Cooked some more and said, "You eat them, for you are a growing lad."
Will ate as many as he could, but soon he had to fly.
He didn't want the tide to turn and leave him high and dry.

We haven't seen him any more. He's married and, you see,
His pretty mermaid wife makes lot of doughnuts for his tea.

PIGS MIGHT FLY

Miss Peggy the Pig asked her Mom, in the sty,
"Do you think, when I'm big, I will learn how to fly?"
Her Momma said, "Darling, please don't be absurd.
You're too roly-poly to act like a bird."

This didn't please Peggy. She made up her mind
That one day she'd leave terra firma behind.
She watched rooks and pigeons to try to learn how
The things that they did could be done by a sow.

A friendly old owl then flew down from a tree
And said to the pig, "If you'll listen to me
You'll settle for what is the very next thing.
It's **almost** like flying to swing on a swing."

So off to the park trotted Peggy, with Owl,
And Sheepdog came too, and some of the Fowl.
"You're bound to regret it," baaed Eunice the Ewe,
"But if you can do it, perhaps I can, too."

The park had three round tyre swings in a row
And Owl said to Peggy, "Come, give it a go."
Poor Peggy wailed, "How do I get in this ring?"
And everyone helped her climb into the swing.

Gently at first, Peggy swung in the tyre,
'Til Sheepdog decided to make it go higher.
He whispered, "I'm gonna give Peggy a scare,"
And pushed her so hard she went up in the air.

Clean out of the tyre Peggy flew, like a bird,
And, very soon after, a loud wail was heard.
"Come help me, please help me. I'm stuck in a bush."
And Sheepdog was sorry about his rough push.

Shaken and scared, Peggy fell to the ground,
And all of her friends quickly gathered around.
They asked, "Are you hurt?" for she'd gone pale with fright.
"Not really," said Peggy, "but Momma was right."

"She's going to tell me that she told me so,
But, just for the record, I want you to know
It wasn't the flying that filled me with fear.
I'm just not equipped with the right landing gear.

From now on, there'll be no more swinging for me.
I'll stay in the farmyard, right where I should be,
But I won't forget, 'til the day that I die,
That once in my lifetime *I really did fly!*"

THE ROLLING STONE

Curvaceous, vivacious Miss Millicent Moss
Had worked as a typist for many a boss,
Whilst middle-aged balding Accountant, Jim Stone,
Preferred to work quietly, all on his own.
But Powers-That-Be, in their cavalier way
Decided Moss, M. should report to Stone, J.

Now Millie habitually stated her mind,
And, signing as 'Stone', one day she outlined
Outstanding defects in Their organization,
And listed alternate economisation.
On reading her memo, Jim cried, "I am dead!"
He gave in his notice and slunk home to bed.

Quite quickly, for all her suggestions made sense,
They summoned Jim Stone, but he'd vanished from thence.
To other positions he made application,
Not knowing his leaving had caused consternation.
He found a new job and, amazed, was accepted
With welcoming arms and improvements expected.

In one or two weeks, when it dawned upon Jim
What great expectations this firm had of him,
He knew he'd need help so, regardless of cost,
He telegraphed Millie, "Without you, I'm lost."
She joined him and quickly concocted a plan
Where many machines could be run by one man.

Jim found he was gaining a bad reputation
For cutting down costs by hard rationalisation.
He tried to escape and sought pastures new,
But Millie soon traced him and came along, too.
She firmly believed that he needed assistance
And dogged all his moves with devoted persistence.

With each moving on, Jim's life savings grew higher.
In fact, he could most afford to retire.

He hated the sight of his pert, bouncy sec,
And wishfully thought about wringing her neck.
But then he was posted to far Bangalore,
And fervently hoped he would see her no more.

Thenceforth, Jim's career was both peaceful and sleepy,
'Til spotted by someone who hated him deeply.
When dawned recognition, as fast as 'twere able,
The rotter sent HQ the following cable:
"Your Bangalore business will be a dead loss
Until Rolling Stone once more gathers his Moss."

ENERGY FROM SAND

From what I read, I understand
There's lots of energy in sand,
Enough to last for years and years
And make oil barons weep hot tears.
Not just on Earth, but out in Space
The sand dunes clutter up the place.
We're running out of power, and
We ought to stick our heads in sand,
(or at least look into it).
We need that energy, my friend,
But first it seems, we'll have to spend
More money than we'll ever earn
Before our clever techies turn
Sand into gold – a miser's bliss –
By man-made photosynthesis.
Extracting power's a lot of troub.
It ain't that easy. That's the rub.
It might not work, and what we'll get
Is just another load of debt,
But please don't let this chance slip by.
We'll never know until we try.

LITTLE MAN

I am the fabric that surrounds you.
Your cradle spins within my unseen tangle
And I hem the rims of crushing, sightless holes.

Little Man, you are afraid of me,
I smell your fear when you reach into me.
For I am dangerous and without pity.

My icy touch becomes your instant death
And no-one hears your screams when I enfold you.
You view the vast domain that lies beyond the stars
And wonder how and when I first began.

Come, little Man, come probe my empty orb,
Show me your nerve and curiosity.
If you will boldly step into my arms
I'll show you wonders through eternity.

PROCRASTINATION

When my Maker made me
What ingredient did he
Omit from my Self
And leave up on the shelf,
While a head full of dreams
And impossible schemes
Led the rest into Life
As a child, then a wife?

I'll finish this tomorrow.

So much for poems. Let's get back to prose. LongRidge wasn't the only writing course that I attended. After moving to South Carolina for a while, I joined the online Christian Writers Group which challenged their writers to write different genres, always observing Christian principles. Most of the following stories came about as a result of membership of that lively writers' group, and I hope you enjoy reading them. I had my tongue in my cheek when I submitted the first story, *A Widow's Weeds*, but it seemed to go down well with my colleagues.

****

A WIDOW'S WEEDS

"Hello, my dear. Still keen on the old gardening?"

Catherine sat back on her haunches, reluctant to face the speaker. It sounded like the little creep she'd hoped never to see again.

She turned her head. It was him.

"Victor! What a surprise. What are you doing in this neck of the woods?"

"I've moved into a place just up the street, my dear. We're neighbours again, just like when I lost my Muriel and you lost your Greg. Imagine my surprise when I saw in the paper that you've lost *another* little husband. Bless me, it's getting to be quite a habit with you. Food poisoning again?"

She struggled to her feet, cursing her weight, and glared at the small, mousy man lounging against her garden shed. She tapped her trowel in the palm of her hand and pursed her lips.

"I don't like that insinuation, Victor."

"Just joshing, my dear. You know me and my little jokes."

"Well, I don't find them funny. Not funny at all. In fact I find them in very bad taste."

"Didn't Greg say that when he drank your elderberry wine?"

What's he getting at?

"That's enough, Victor. My Greg's death was as natural as your Muriel's."

"Of course it was, my dear."

Catherine clamped a hand over her mouth to stifle her reaction.

Victor strolled down the path towards her. He smiled a horrid, sly, conspiratorial smile, and her heart missed a beat.

He's found out about Greg. But I know about Muriel. That makes us even.

"As I was saying, my dear, you've been very careless with your husbands. How many is that so far? Um, let's see. Three, isn't it?"

Three? Omigod. How did he ever find out about Alf?

"How can you say such a thing, Victor? Fate was cruel taking Jim away so soon after Greg." She gave a little sniff. "By the way, I don't know where you get three from."

"I'm thinking about Alf. It was Alf, wasn't it? The one who disappeared? Ran off with a singer, I heard. Odd that. Very odd. Him a lay preacher and you such a fine, handsome woman."

He's fishing. He can't possibly know about Alf. It was so long ago. What's he up to? Whatever it is, I wish he'd stop pussy-footing around.

"I've been meaning to call on you, my dear, but then Jim died and I didn't want to intrude while you were still wearing your widow's weeds. Black suits you, by the way. The trouble is, my dear, I can't wait any longer. I need to ask you something, but don't quite know how to put it."

Now we come to it. "Spit it out, Victor."

"Don't be like that, my dear. It's just that somehow I've got behind with some bills. A long way behind. I wondered if you could help me out."

"How much?"

"Two thousand."

Catherine dropped her trowel.

"But one thousand would get me off the hook."

"What happened to Muriel's insurance?"

"That didn't last long, my dear. Not long at all."

This has got to be nipped in the bud. Right now.

She picked at the fingertips of her gardening gloves in mock anxiety, and then looked under her eyelids at Victor, making sure he saw her, before averting her gaze.

"Well, of course I'll help if I can." She bit into the grubby forefinger of her glove, spat out a morsel of dirt and clasped her hands. "But I don't have that kind of money in the house. I'll have to go to the bank for some this afternoon. Will that be all right?"

"Some? How much?"

She gnawed her glove again. "I can get five hundred today, but I'll have to cash in some securities for the rest. That'll take a few days."

"Um, I'm being hounded. Can I come back tonight for the five hundred? Say, about seven?"

"Yes." She bent to pick up her trowel, revealing her cleavage. "I don't suppose you'd care to have supper with me while you're here? We could talk about old times."

Victor's eyes gleamed, and he licked his lips.

"Go on. I dare you. I won't give you any of Greg's wine." She forced a coquettish smile.

Victor grinned. "I've a good, strong constitution, my dear, and I'm not afraid of anything you can cook up. But I will say no to chicken. Especially frozen chicken. Afraid of salmonella, you understand."

"I understand perfectly, Victor."

"All right, my dear. Then I'll be off. See you at seven."

Catherine watched him trot briskly down the path toward the gate. Then she puffed after him and clutched his arm.

"Er, Victor. You will be discreet, won't you? I mean, Jim's not long passed away. What will the neighbours think?"

"I'll be the soul of discretion, my dear."

She made sure the gate was securely locked before she ripped off her gloves and tossed them into the shed, along with her gardening tools. Then she wandered along the little path that wound between her beloved plants, and looked around.

I'll make a chef's salad with monkshood and hemlock, mixed with lettuce and spinach, and smother it in dressing. The rhubarb looks just right. I'm glad I didn't leave the root behind when I moved. I'll make a nice rhubarb crumble topped with ice cream and some of Jim's peanuts. Chopped of course.

Now, where did I put that carpet runner I used to drag Alf out of the house? He had it coming. Him with his text for every occasion – and his stinginess. Marking the sherry bottle and kicking up a fuss just because I borrowed a few dollars out of his pants now and then. I can still hear him hollering 'Be sure your sins will find you out'. Well, he hollered one time too many. Now Victor can join him in the quarry.

Shame Greg lost his job and was such a drain on my finances. He was quite a nice fellow. Still, the insurance made up for losing him. And Jim was an out and out liar – telling me he had all that money when he hadn't. But all's well that ends well. Thank you, Jim, for pigging on those peanuts. You saved me months of work.

She stroked the leaves of a sturdy hemlock plant that was nearly hidden under a straggling bush. "You'll do nicely," she murmured. "Now, where's the monkshood?"

--o—

Sweat dripped off Catherine by the time she picked Victor up in her arms, like a big baby, and dropped him into the back of her purring minivan. He hadn't eaten as much as she'd hoped, and it took hours before the weeds affected him and he doubled up in agony.

Alf wasn't half this trouble. But then this house doesn't have hardwood floors like the old one did. It was a breeze dragging Alf to the back door on that bit of runner. Thank heaven Greg and Jim both died in hospital.

She backed the Windstar cautiously out of the driveway and peered into her mirror.

What's going on up the road? That looks like a police van and an ambulance. But they haven't got their lights on. It can't be serious.

"Oh, shoot! Which way do I go?"

Don't panic. Go back to the old house. No. Take the next left and get onto the ring road.

Sc-r-e-e-ch.

Damn. Forgot that corner was so sharp.

"I'm going the wrong way! What'll I do? What'll I do?"

Take the next right. Then right again.

Sc-r-e-e-ch. Sc-r-e-e-ch.

"Omigod! That cop car's following me! And the ambulance! What'll I do? What'll I do?"

Pull yourself together. You're imagining it. Pull over and let them go by.

"I'm not imagining it. He's got his lights on. Omigod! Omigod!"

Put your foot down. Shake him off.

Sc-r-e-e-ech. Sc-r-e-e-e-e-e-e-ch.

Whee, wheee, wheee.

Catherine pulled over. Her tires bruised the curb. She dropped her head onto the wheel.

Tap, tap.

She lifted her head and wound down the window. "What is it, officer?"

"Pull the lever so we can open the back doors. Then get out. Come on. Come on. I haven't got all night."

"You're harassing me. You're not allowed to do this."

"You're not allowed to kill people."

"What!"

While Catherine heaved herself out of the van, the police officer beckoned the ambulance. It came close, hemming them both in.

The cop's partner ran to pull the back doors of the van wide open, while two paramedics maneuvered a gurney out of the ambulance. It took barely a minute to haul Victor out of the van, straighten him out of the fetal position, strap him onto the gurney, and wheel him into the ambulance.

"Don't hang about," ordered the officer standing next to Catherine.

The ambulance raced away, its lights flashing.

The cop's partner strode back to them and stood on the other side of Catherine.

She glanced from one officer to the other. "How did you know he was in there?"

"He was bugged, ma'am."

"You mean you knew where he was and what he was doing all the time?"

"That's right, ma'am."

"Why? You've got no evidence against me---"

"Oh, yes we do, ma'am. We've got the forensic reports on the contents of Alf's stomach. He was my brother, by the way. We've suspected you since we found his body at the bottom of Thorncross Quarry. We've also got forensics on Greg Walker and Jim Burton."

"I didn't kill Jim. It was the peanuts."

"Partly. Soon we'll know what's in Victor's stomach. Plus we've got that incriminating meal, sitting nice and handy on your living room table."

"Victor's as bad as me. He killed his wife, Muriel."

"Did you ever meet Muriel?"

"N-no. He was visiting her while I was visiting Greg. He invited me to her funeral."

"Knowing full well you wouldn't go. There was no Muriel, ma'am. Victor is an undercover police officer. He established a friendship with you when Walker fell sick, but lost your trail when you moved suddenly. Then he saw Jim Burton's obituary and tracked you down. He's a brave man. There's not many that would willingly eat poisonous weeds to get a conviction."

"So he wanted me to invite him to supper."

"That's correct, ma'am."

"I'll read her rights, Earl. Then you can drive us back to the station."

Alf's brother intoned the words Catherine had heard so many times while watching C.S.I.

"Have you anything to say?" he concluded.

She shook her head.

But I know what Alf would have said. He'd have said, "Be sure your sins will find you out." And they have.

****

From this point, I will let the stories follow each other without introduction, as they ramble amongst humour, horror, family matters, and science-fiction. Most of them were written a long time ago, so you won't come across many computers or other technological advances. Read on and enjoy!

MARGUERITE'S COMEUPPANCE

Judith saw the determination in the younger woman's eyes when she took the dictation tape. *You're after my job*, she thought. *But hard luck, sister. You're not Mr. Prescott's type.*

"See me if you have any questions," she told Marguerite, and went back to her own tape.

Marguerite was curvy, with artfully tangled brown hair and true blue eyes that were fringed by long, thick eyelashes which she continually fluttered. She didn't walk. She danced. And while she danced, she waved her arms as if trying to keep her balance. She had an engaging smile that she flashed to escape trouble after flouting authority – something she did frequently.

Judith, on the other hand, was tall, trim, and twice Marguerite's age. Years in the sun had embedded creases round her laughing brown eyes. She kept her blonde hair short, closely clipped at the back, and, to hide her bony limbs, she wore long-sleeved shirts over dark pants. She ran the office smoothly and efficiently, in spite of Marguerite's efforts at disruption.

Marguerite waltzed back to her desk near the door of the office suite where she also manned the switchboard and greeted clients. For a while the office was quiet except for the clicking of keyboards. But then Judith caught a whiff of perfume. Marguerite had snuck up behind her and was about to enter Mr. Prescott's office.

"What is it?" Judith asked, swiveling round to halt the intruder.

"I'll only be a teensy minute," Marguerite said, dodging Judith's arm, and skipping into the hallowed office.

He's not impressed, Judith thought. She watched the Senior Partner regard Marguerite stonily when she leaned forward provocatively, holding out a sheet of paper in both hands.

"I'm afraid you're guilty of tautology here, sir," she heard Marguerite say. "Do you agree with my correction?"

Mr. Prescott gave the sheet a cursory glance. "Yes. Thank you."

"Lucky I checked," Marguerite said, triumphantly, on her way back to her desk.

Judith thought, while gritting her teeth, *you'll get your comeuppance one of these days*.

"Mrs. Thomas," Mr. Prescott called.

"Where was Mrs. Everett last Friday?" he growled when Judith went into his office.

"She said she had to join her husband on an important engagement."

"Didn't I make it crystal clear that no typist could be absent on deed-checking day?"

"Yes, you did, but---"

"Were any deeds out of place?" he interrupted, testily.

"Just one packet, in Hunt -v- Hunt."

"Tell Mrs. Everett to check that shelf again."

"But *I* did that section."

Mr. Prescott pursed his lips. "Why is she working on my files?"

"She wanted something to do. The board was quiet and I had the most tapes."

"Hmmph! Take her off my work and give her something else."

Judith left the old grouch and went into the adjoining office, occupied by John Masters. His father had, with Richard Prescott, founded the firm. He was a pleasant, well-built man who worked in his shirtsleeves, whatever the weather.

"What's up?" he asked, after Judith apologised for interrupting him.

"Do you have a tape or anything for Marguerite to do?"

John swung round to the precariously-stacked pile of files behind him. "She can copy the tagged sheets in this file. I've got to give discovery soon."

Judith beckoned Marguerite from John's open doorway.

She knew Marguerite wouldn't mind using the copier because, while at the big Xerox, situated as it was in the center of the office, Marguerite could overhear the other typists' conversations. She had an annoying habit of butting in to claim to have done something bigger, better or worse. For example, after one typist's car got stuck in a flood, Marguerite said she had aquaplaned – in a Jaguar, no less – on a busy road until she was lucky enough (Marguerite was always 'lucky' one way or another) to have driven over a fallen branch which broke the hold of the water.

Swinging her hips gracefully, Marguerite wove her way between the desks, until she reached John's office.

Judith left her with him and returned to her desk, anxious to get on with her work. She was about to plug in her earphones when she heard John ask:

"So where were you on Friday? We missed you."

Marguerite accepted the file he held out to her, and laughed gaily. "It was our wedding anniversary, and Roger took me out for the day."

Judith got up from her chair. *That was no important engagement*, she thought, angrily. She marched into John's office.

"Where did you go?" John asked.

"Fishing," Marguerite stage-whispered "It was my first time ever." She carried on speaking in her usual clear voice. "I was lucky enough to catch a chub. Roger said it was a good size. Nearly two pounds."

John frowned and shot a glance at his calendar. "Grafham or Rutland Water, I suppose."

She laughed. "Oh, no. We found a nice spot on the river bank. I nearly fell in when my rod came apart. Lucky for me, Roger managed to grab hold of it."

John stiffened. "You can't go fishing now, except on a stocked lake. It's still close season."

Marguerite stared at him. Then fear crept into her eyes. A guilty blush raced up her neck and onto her cheeks when she realised she'd been caught in a lie.

"But, but ...," she stammered.

Judith felt someone behind her, and heard an icy voice command, "Mrs. Everett. Step into my office."

While watching Mr. Prescott rebuke a crestfallen Marguerite, Judith knew he would be threatening dismissal, but she also knew the office would be a poorer place without the ambitious young woman. Marguerite captivated clients with her smile and attentive manner and her work, once she settled down to it, was always good.

I'll give her one more chance, Judith decided. *Maybe this time she'll learn her lesson.*

But, in her heart, she doubted it.

****

ON THE FLY

The dirty dog dropped his disgusting dump right in the middle of my deck. The stink wafted in through the open French windows and I thanked the Lord for flyscreens.

Zee-ee-ee-ee-ee-ee.

A bluebottle zipped past my ear. How had he gotten in?

Aha! Several others of his ilk crawled towards a hole in the patio screen.

I waddled over to it – I'm a smidgeon overweight – and shut the glass door. Then, trusty fly swatter in hand, I hunted the fly.

Zee-ee-ee-ee-ee-ee.

He dived onto my head and buzzed like a road drill in my hair.

Geroff! I swung an angry arm upwards and knocked off my glasses.

Zee-ee-ee-ee-ee-ee.

The blasted bluey was laughing at me.

"I'll let you settle," I said to myself. "I'll make myself a cuppa and swat you when you're not looking."

The fly sat on my draining board, preening himself in his iridescent green glory, while I poured boiling water onto my teabag, and then added milk and sugar.

Testing me, he flew towards the sugar.

I flapped a hand – the one holding the spoon. As a result, it flew into space and landed on the floor. Ouch! While retrieving it, I hit my head on the sink front when I straightened up.

Zee-ee-ee-ee-ee-ee.

"I'll get you," I shouted. "You flying fragment of filth!"

The fly soared onto the ceiling fan and watched me snatch the swatter off the worktop.

I reached up, while humming the *Blue Danube*.

Whap, whap, whap, whap, swish, swish, whap, whap.

Missed him. I tried again.

Whap, whap, whap, whap. Drat it. Missed him again.

I tried fencing.

Whap, whap, whap, and lunge. Whap, whap, whap, and lunge.

He dodged all my moves. He was enjoying this, I could tell.

"Stay still!" I shouted. I leapt into the air and whacked the fan, only to land awkwardly and heard the back seam of my shorts rip.

Zee-ee-ee-ee-ee-ee.

Mad as hell, I scrambled to my feet. Then, with a dazzling display of dexterity, I flung the swatter at the fly. The makeshift missile caught him in the midriff.

"Touché" I yelled.

Although grievously wounded, my opponent didn't fall: he flew in unsteady circles around the fan.

I wilted. The fight had exhausted me and I needed a drink. Cradling my cup in both hands, I lifted it towards my lips.

The fly spiraled downwards in diminishing circles. I watched him until my eyes crossed. Then, plop! He fell straight into my tea.

You know about momentum, don't you? How you can't stop a body once it's gotten up speed?

My lusting lips, fully extended, were about to slurp when the crippled carcass splashed tea into my mouth. I felt a lump slide down my throat.

"Aaarrgh!" I yelled, and rushed to the bathroom.

I guess you could call that a draw.

****

LITTLE DEVIL

I'm sliding off Mum's lap 'cos of her bump. She's feeling awful sick today, so she's come to see her doctor. I had to come, too, 'cos no-one wants to look after me.

If I stick my legs out, I can reach the nasty man's pants. Hee, hee. I put mud on them. He's sitting next to Mum. That was my chair. I put my cars on the chairs next to Mum. Now I have to put them on the floor. But that's all right. I can make them scrape.

Everybody's looking at Mum because they hate the noise, and she says, "What are we going to do with you?" like she was two people.

I want to go home. We've been waiting for **ever**. The desk lady said we missed our turn. Mum said I'd made her late. I lost my red car. It's my favourite. Then Mum said she didn't feel good and the desk lady said she'd fit us in. I like the desk lady.

Loads of people are in here. A fat lady came to sit next to Mum and another lady said, "Don't make him cry. For God's sake don't make him cry."

I don't like her. She lives near us and she's mean. She smacked me when Mum asked her to look after me once. Said I broke her cat's leg.

But the fat lady sat down anyway, and I cried. I cried and cried 'til Mum picked me up. I put my arms round her neck and kissed her. She gave me a lollipop. I always kiss her when I want something.

I was sucking my lollipop when the nasty man came in and saw my other chair. He had a bad foot. He made angry eyes when I leaned over the seat, so he couldn't have it. Mum dragged me off and put me on her lap. She held me real tight round my tummy. Then the nasty man bumped the chair away 'cos I kicked him.

He's looking at the mud on his pants now. He's gonna say something to Mum. But Mum's making a funny noise, like she's gargling.

Yay! She let me go! I can run!

The desk lady catches me and I hit her. She doesn't say anything. She's looking at Mum.

Everybody's looking at Mum.

Mum's sitting all floppy with her legs open. She smells bad, like she farted.

The mean lady says, "She's a single mum. Doesn't have a soul in the world except ..." She nods at me. "She claims he was an act of God 'cause she never had sex. If you believe that, you'll believe anything. Don't know who'll look after him now and, what's more, I don't care. He's a right little devil."

The nasty man is looking at Mom, and screwing up his face like he's eaten something bad.

"I think she's dead!" he says.

I pretend to cry.

The desk lady bends down and picks me up.

"Dear Lord, what are we going to do with you?" she asks.

I like the desk lady. I put my arms round her neck and hug her tight. I kiss her and say, "Are you my new Mummy?"

Her eyes go all funny, and I kiss her again.

"Of course, honey," she says.

"And my new bruvver?"

"Brother?"

I lift my head and look at my old Mum. Something slimy and bloody is sliding out between her legs. It lands on the floor with a wet plop, and splashes the nasty man's pants. I snuggle against the desk lady and stroke her cheek.

The desk lady stares at the thing wriggling on the floor.

I nuzzle my nose on her cheek and she shivers.

She likes that. I do it again and kiss her.

"Of course, honey," she says.

****

THE YELLOW BUTTERFLY

I had the old nightmare again last night.

The yellow butterfly, in its fragile, fiery beauty, fluttered and swooped through tumbling shadows. Its stench filled my nostrils yet again, and the haunting scream echoed around me. Why can't I forget something that happened so long ago?

It was autumn in 1940, the day after my little sister turned three. I was four and tended to boss her. We were playing in the long, wet grass in our untidy front garden. Our bare toes were cold in our sandals and our coats were soaked with dew. We kept away from the hedge, hung with spider webs that sparkled in the cold sunlight. I didn't like spiders. I liked butterflies.

Clip clop, clip clop. A horse came plodding down the road, and we ran to the gate.

Someone was getting coal. The horse stopped at our neighbour's house. Mum called the lady who lived there a busybody. She said Mum was a slut and not fit to have kids. We spotted the busybody coming down her path with a little girl who was nearly as old as me.

"Don't go near them, Maggie. You'll catch the impetigo," we heard her say.

The coalman had a shiny leather pad on his back. He grunted when he strained to lift one of the hundredweight bags onto his shoulders before trudging towards their coal shed. We ran out of the gate and patted the big horse. He nudged us, looking for sugar, and his breath steamed in the cold air. We wanted sugar, too, but it was on ration.

When the coalman hoisted the next bag, he stumbled and lots of shiny black coal spilled onto the pavement. We ran to pick it up, using our coats to hold it, until I saw the busybody watching us. She frowned and I dropped mine. But then she shook her head sadly, and gave me a little smile.

"You can have it. Go get a bucket," she said.

We scampered indoors and grabbed the big pail that Mum used to steep our baby brother's nappies. Our eldest sister stopped playing in the kitchen and came out, too. She should have been at school because she was five, but Mum said she needed her at home.

We collected the big pieces and dropped them in the pail, and then used our hands to scoop up the rest. Gritty black dust fell into our sandals and down our coats, but they were dirty anyway. We dragged the pail towards our house, scraping a channel through the soft earth, uprooting weeds and bruising our legs.

Mum took the bucket at the door and kicked it near to the hearth. Her belly was big and round and she said she shouldn't lift anything heavy. Then she went back to close the front door, but didn't say thank you, or even look at the busybody who was watching over the hedge.

After that, we played indoors. It grew dark, except in the kitchen where the oil lamp burned. Mum laid a fire in the living room but it wouldn't catch, so she soaked newspaper in paraffin and stuffed it under the firewood. Before we had to leave London and came to live in the country, Dad always lit the fires. He went to France a year ago to fight, and I missed him.

The wood began to burn and flames licked round the lumps of coal. Mum said it was poor coal, but beggars can't be choosers.

My tummy rumbled. I hoped there'd be some brown jelly on my bread and dripping. The salty jelly stung when it got in the sores round my mouth, but Mum said salt would make them heal quicker. My little sister sat on the floor with me, in front of the fire. While we waited for our supper we took off our sandals and shook the coal dust out of them, adding to the dirt on the filthy floor. We stretched our toes towards the hearth to warm them.

Mum came in and gave us bread and dripping, and then lit a candle on the table. It made shadows dance on the walls and black smoke curled from the tip of the flame.

Then she swore at the smouldering fire and lodged a big tin lid in the grate. That lid broke off one of Daddy's boxes, and Mum kept it. She said it created a draught and made the fire burn better. She told us not to touch the lid, and then left us sitting on the floor while she went back to the kitchen.

The fire began to spit and crackle and we felt the lovely heat. I hoped we could sleep on the couch in front of the fire, and not go upstairs to bed. It was cold and dark up there. Me and my sisters slept on a lumpy, smelly mattress on the floor. We all wet the bed. The blankets reeked of pee, too. In the dark we could hear mice squeak and sometimes they ran over us. One night I felt a big lump under the blanket. It was cold and stiff and I chucked it away, and I heard it hit the wall. I didn't hurt it because it was dead already.

The fire is roaring and the room is really warm now. I scratch my head because the heat has woken up the fleas. The edge of the lid nearest my little sister is glowing red. Suddenly something in the fire hits the lid with a loud ping. Slowly, ever so slowly it seems, the lid topples forward and we watch bright sparks leaping up the chimney.

The lid fell mostly onto the tiled hearth but the red-hot edge landed on my little sister's foot. I grabbed my sandal and flipped the lid up, while dragging her foot away. A horrid smell filled the room. My stomach heaved, and I choked, sudden vomit stinging my nose and throat.

Without the draught, the fire died and dark shadows stole around us. My little sister stared at her foot. A flame sprang out of it, looking like a bright yellow butterfly, its wings erect and quivering. Then the wings spread and covered her tiny foot. They fluttered up and down as if getting ready to fly away.

Someone screamed, a shrill, piercing scream that can only come from someone who is terrified. Darkness wrapped around the scream. I don't remember what happened after that.

Seventy years later, my sister doesn't remember how she got the scar across her foot. My scar is just as permanent, but you can't see it. On restless nights, the yellow butterfly flits into my dreams, trailing its stink of burning flesh. As it flutters away, the scream pulses in my head, making my heart thump. I bury my face in my pillow and cover my ears.

I don't like butterflies any more. I prefer spiders.

****

THE DEVIL'S PUNCHBOWL

Shania always hated leaving work late, especially in the winter when darkness fell early. In the north, where she lived, winter always came early and lasted longer. It was about time they changed the calendar, she thought, so that April heralded spring and May saw it leave. Summer would last through June and July, and fall would arrive in August, to creep away in September. That left October through March as winter.

She'd had no choice but to work late after a colleague left the office in a snit due to a misunderstanding. It meant that Shania had to finish backing-up the day's work on her own – always a long process, even with two of them. And, to make it worse, tonight was Halloween.

The back-up took until eight o'clock. On her way down to the lobby, she glanced out of the windows. Her car would be isolated in the parking lot, and she bet there would be idiots lurking out there, wearing hideous masks and scary outfits, who would have "fun" with her.

She was right. There they were – a gang of noisy teenagers, grey ghosts trailing yards of spider web stuff – horsing around in the dark with another group of silver skeletons whose red eyes glowed in their grotesque faces, their clawed hands swinging blood-daubed scythes.

Worse still, it was misty.

Her car couldn't cope with mist. It always fogged up and she had to open her window. Like the tires on her car, the wipers needed replacing. They left streaks she couldn't see through. She sighed and hunched her hoodie over her head.

"I'll walk over with you."

Shania turned gratefully to Ike, the late-shift manager, and then recoiled. He was wearing a horrid rubber mask. "Please take it off," she begged him.

He obliged and walked with her to her car, after which he approached the teenagers and told them to keep the noise down.

Shania saw him put the mask back on, and shook her head. He wasn't so much telling them off as joining in with them. Some guys never grow up.

In no time, it seemed, she had left the brightness of the town behind her. After the lights advertising roadside businesses receded, the only colors to break the blackness were occasional traffic lights. The mist spangled red, green or amber spheres across the windscreen, blurring her vision. Then she found herself driving through a desolate abandoned half-completed housing complex. The developer had bought the land at a sky-high price. The bubble had burst and he had been ruined.

She glanced at her odometer. Ten miles down, twenty more to go to her home in the middle of nowhere. It was either make this journey twice a day or be unemployed again. She'd had enough of that. The job didn't pay much, but at least she had a job, unlike so many people in the town where she lived. She put her foot down to get home faster.

As Shania had foreseen, the windscreen began to fog up. She cracked the window an inch and felt the damp seep into the car. The road ahead ran straight as a die. There were two miles to go before she reached the narrow wooden bridge over the Devil's Punchbowl, and three miles beyond that she would reach the turn-off to home and security. Then she could sleep and unwind before the early morning trip back to town. But that would be in daylight and she would enjoy the ride. It was only at night when there was no moon that she was assailed by unreasonable fears and her stomach knotted.

The wind picked up, and she felt it ruffle her hair. The wispy mist parted, allowing the car to nose through it. She cut her speed, although she longed to keep her foot down. The bridge ahead would be slippery. She didn't want to skid and end up in the deep oval lake below, the way so many others had over the years.

One mile to Devil's Punchbowl. Bile rose in her throat. She could just make out the outline of the tiny church half-a-mile ahead, off to her right. Gravestones littered the ground around it: grey blobs in the mist. Nobody attended that church on a regular basis. It existed only as a place to hold funeral services for the unfortunates who fell, slid or jumped into the murky waters of the Devil's Punchbowl.

The hair on the back of her neck bristled when she drew near to the graveyard, and her heart thumped. Was it her imagination or had the wind started moaning? Then her eyes played tricks. Shapes formed around her, sliding in and out of the mist. They stretched ghostly arms towards the car.

Were the dead rising? They were supposed to do that on Halloween.

Shania's heart thumped louder, faster.

"Quit it," she told herself.

Relief drenched her when the car passed the graveyard and approached the bridge.

But then the car began to slide.

Not sideways. Down, down, down.

She flipped on her main beam. Only yards ahead the center span of the bridge had collapsed. She was driving into water, silent and threatening, only yards away.

She screamed. Shaking violently, she changed gears and tried to drive backwards. She had gained a few feet when the engine spluttered and died. She was sliding forward again. She yanked on the brakes and prayed they would hold.

And they did – almost. The still water inched nearer and nearer.

She turned the key again before she glanced at the gas gauge.

Empty!

She'd intended to fill up on her way into work, but didn't have enough time, and had forgotten.

Then the headlights died. Blackness settled on her like a monster smothering its prey.

The water reached the front wheel arch.

Panic seized her and she started to cry.

She had to get out.

She found her flashlight and felt for the door lever, but her hand froze on it.

Long, green fingernails tapped outside her window.

She jabbed the window button to close the gap, but the moldy fingers prevented the glass from reaching the frame. They pushed the window down.

Freezing water drenched and numbed her.

She lost all will to resist.

--o--

Two weeks later, her workmates gathered at the tiny church and mourned the passing of another victim of the Devil's Punchbowl.

****

A MIS–TAKEN CASE OF IDENTITY

It wasn't until the key refused to turn that I noticed the zipper ends weren't under the handle, where I always put them. And that scratch on the side wasn't there when I checked in.

Would you believe it? I've picked up the wrong case. Mine must still be at Logan.

I thought back to when I stood by the carousel. My fellow travelers formed a solid fence around its perimeter. I spotted my case coming, squeezed to the front and leaned in, only to be knocked back by a guy who lunged onto the carousel.

"Sorry," he mumbled. He grabbed a case and moved away.

"Is this yours?" A tall, skinny man had pulled my case off the belt.

"Oh, yes. Thanks. Thanks."

He rolled it towards me, and then dived back into the scrimmage.

--o--

I sat back on my haunches and looked for signs of the rightful owner's identity.

Nothing.

O-o-okay. Where are my spare keys?

I have a big bunch of spare keys, having worn out suitcases the way other women wear out shoes. The third one on the ring opened the lock. I pushed the lid open and flexed my fingers, ready to rummage.

And blinked.

There, held down by the cross-over straps, and placed precisely in the center of a snowy white towel, was a notice.

In 96-point black letters on thick white paper it proclaimed:

YOU HAVE THE WRONG CASE.

Underneath that bold statement was an invitation to contact Walter by phone or e-mail.

The neatly-tucked white towel irritated me. I thought of my own case, stuffed with bikinis that had doubled as underwear, crumpled tee shirts, fraying towels and dog-eared paperbacks. The holiday had been relaxing, but boring with no-one else for company. I wanted to rumple Walter's case, move everything around, like Laura and the teatowels in *Sleeping With The Enemy*.

But it's not my case.

He'll never know. I'll put everything back.

The temptation was too strong. I undid the cross-over straps and tossed the towel onto the lid, revealing several neatly-labeled manila folders.

I bet Walter's an accountant.

No, not an accountant. An actor, or a nutcase.

Underneath the folders was another towel. Underneath that, the case was divided into four sections, separated by pieces of plywood. Each section contained an assortment of clothes and, sticky-taped onto the top garment in each section, was an obviously fake passport.

What's with this guy? Does he have a personality disorder?

The top left section held two garments – a dark bulky sweatshirt and matching sweats. Three fake passports lay on top of the sweatshirt. The top one was for the EU. Beneath that was an Australian one, and under that, a Russian. A cardboard cut-out of a pistol poked out of the sweat pants' pocket.

Intrigued, I opened the passports in turn. Each one had a similar photograph of a dishy young man, identified as Walter Bourne.

I giggled. Talk about living out a fantasy.

The passport in the top right section belonged to a Walter Proteus. He stared at me solemnly from the details page. On his head, a silver crown perched at an angle over straggly locks that were decorated with strands of seaweed. An eel snaked over his bare shoulders. Proteus's clothes consisted of three mankinis, all in aqua blue, and a pair of flippers.

Why choose to be Proteus? Then I remembered that Proteus could change into another being whenever he wanted to.

I turned to the section below Proteus, and felt cheated when I found nothing special, but then I opened four fake passports. Stapled inside were photos of Walter Donald Trump, Walter George Bush, Walter Paul McCartney, and Walter Charles Windsor.

In the last section, bewigged Walter Blakeney's passport sat atop a frilled shirt and slim-cut suede pants. A large washbag ornamented with pimpernels held soap, bottles of aftershave, perfume and lace-edged handkerchiefs.

Walter was something else. I decided I had to meet him in person and searched for the piece of paper that gave his e-mail address. However, right then my doorbell rang.

Walter stood on the doorstep, my suitcase beside him. "I found your name and address on the tag," he said, "so I came to do a swap."

I grabbed his hand, pulled him into the lounge, and pointed to his case.

"Explain yourself. Who are you? Really?"

He laughed. "I'm an accountant."

"Thought so."

"But in my spare time, I write books under a pseudonym. Have you heard of Don Counter?"

"No, sorry."

Walter sighed. "I always play this game when I travel. Just for fun. You see, my real name is..."

He reached inside his back pocket, pulled out his driving license and showed it to me.

Walter Mitty.

His real name was Walter Mitty.

****

UNSPILLED MILK

"Are we there yet?"

Josh barely heard Sergei's whispered favourite joke. He hovered beside his sick companion and loosened, very slightly, the straps keeping the cosmonaut in his bunk. He shook his head. "Not yet, Sergei, but we soon will be. Only two more days, buddy. Half a million miles, and we'll re-enter Earth's atmosphere."

"It's been so long."

"You can say that again. Seven months non-stop. But it's nearly over."

Sergei's chest heaved in his spacesuit, and a sigh wheezed through his colorless lips.

Josh eyed him anxiously. Don't die on me now, he thought. Not now we're so near home.

He glanced at the body bag strapped to the wall. It had been put there 'just in case'. During lift-off, Josh had prayed that Sergei, who was exhibiting early signs, would stave off the sickness that had killed the other members of their team. Why was only their base affected? It wasn't as if they'd been on Mars the longest. Was it something to do with the gases that seeped out of the permafrost?

And why hadn't it affected him? Thank the Lord it hadn't, but it had been a long, lonely journey with Sergei sleeping in his silently spinning bunk most of the time while their comrades' bodies hung in tightly-sealed bags in the loaded-to-the-gills cargo section. Cargo was all this clumsy earth return vehicle was supposed to carry, but the designers had been persuaded to include cramped facilities for two astronauts, in case of emergency. An emergency like this. If only Sergei hadn't been sick, both of them could have spent weeks in suspended animation, and life would have been so much easier. The daily routine was crushing him.

112

Josh snapped out of his reverie. It was time to see to Sergei. He loosened all the straps holding the sick man's body, turned him onto his side, unsnapped the suit's back flap and removed the damp diaper. Then he carefully fitted a new one in place.

There was barely enough room in the waste container for the used diaper, but everything had to be kept for examination. He massaged Sergei's lower back as best he could before snapping the flap and gently turning the wasted man onto his back. He tightened the chest straps and reached for Sergei's legs.

"On yer bike, Serge, me old buddy. A hundred pushes, and you can have your milk."

Sergei smiled feebly and then turned his head to one side.

"Stars. Let me see the stars."

Josh hesitated. What were the chances of a random burst of deadly radiation entering their small cabin? That would finish them both off – if not immediately, it would later.

Sergei's eyes pleaded with him.

"Just while you're doing your exercises, buddy."

Josh reached up to tug at a hinged panel, turning it back like a page in a book, and clipped it flat against the cabin wall. A clear plastic block, two inches thick, separated them from the fatal embrace of outer space while their tiny ship streaked through stars pasted onto never-ending blackness. Some twinkled brightly, steadily. Others burst with brilliant energy and suddenly died. A shower of sparkling meteorites zoomed into view.

"Please don't let them hit us, Lord," breathed Josh.

Sergei sighed with pleasure. "The heavens tell out the glory of God," he recited slowly.

Josh turned from the window and floated to Sergei's bunk where he grasped his ankles. It was hard work moving his comrade's legs as if he were pedaling a bike. Sergei focused on heaven's pageantry, unable to help. Josh's back ached, his fingers became numb, and his head pounded. Was he succumbing to the sickness, too? It wouldn't be surprising after the months of confinement in this small space with Sergei.

What if I feel worse tomorrow? What if I don't make the right approach? What if I screw up re-entry and miss Earth altogether? We will die and drift forever among the stars.

Josh shuddered and tried to pull himself together. Maybe it wasn't the sickness. Maybe he was just plumb worn out with the effort of looking after Sergei. Maybe all he needed was a good, long nap. But Sergei had to have his drink before Josh could drift into undemanding sleep in his own narrow bunk.

After securing his friend's legs, Josh floated to the food supply cabinet. Four small bottles of special milk huddled together in the middle of the long center shelf – all that was left. One each, for today and tomorrow. He lifted one of the small bottles and closed the cupboard door. After shaking the bottle, he propelled himself towards Sergei, while trying to undo the cap with unfeeling fingers.

Bump! He collided with Sergei's bunk.

It was a gentle bump but enough to jerk his arm.

The cap opened.

Milk floated out. It swirled above him in beads like a shattered necklace.

Josh stared in horror as the slowly circling drops broke into ever smaller drops.

In frustration, he threw himself down to the floor, where he knelt beside Sergei's dangling arm. "Why did you let that happen, Lord?" he raged. "Why? How can I share mine when we both need a full bottle. Why, Lord? Why? Oh, Lord, I've tried so hard."

He felt a nudge against his shoulder.

Sergei was trying to lift his arm. What for?

Scarcely able to believe his eyes, Josh watched the sick man bend his elbow and slowly, oh so slowly, lift his forearm. He put a supporting hand under Sergei's elbow. There seemed to be nothing solid inside the spacesuit. Then he lifted the arm until it was high enough to lie on Sergei's chest.

"Okay, buddy. You've got your arm. What do you want it for?"

Sergei smiled. Josh watched him lift his hand and point at a bead of milk that was slowly coming towards him. Up, up, went the thin hand. Nearer and nearer drifted the drop of milk until it landed, like a gleaming pearl, on Sergei's forefinger. With a thumping heart, Josh helped to direct the finger to Sergei's mouth, half-hidden by his bushy beard. Then a grey, questing tongue reached out to capture the prize.

Josh bowed his head, grateful that in his anguish he hadn't cracked the edible bottle.

"Thank you, Lord," he whispered. "I know what to do now."

Holding the bottle in one hand, and steering himself with his feet and free hand, Josh floated around the cabin, guiding drifting drops of milk into the bottle while making sure none of them landed on himself or any other surface. Each time he captured one, he moved his thumb onto the top of the bottle to keep the precious liquid inside. His arm ached and his hand shook, but gradually the bottle filled. Every now and then he glanced back at Sergei who was watching him intently. Finally, cradling the full bottle in both hands, he asked, "Can you see any more, old buddy?"

The sick man shook his head, lifted a trembling congratulatory thumb, and smiled.

Carefully, not wanting to spill the milk again, Josh held the bottle out. He kept his thumb in place until Sergei's mouth closed around it, and long whiskers tickled his fingers. That beard would need trimming tomorrow before he put on Sergei's helmet, ready for re-entry.

When Sergei was holding the bottle properly, Josh left him and moved to the window to have one last look at the stars. He closed the panel and eased himself onto his bunk where he listened to his friend crunching the shell of the bottle.

While Josh mechanically pushed his tired legs, he thought over what had just happened. If that milk had been spilled on Earth, no-one could have retrieved it, let alone drink it. When the liquid hit the ground it would have been contaminated, infiltrated by a legion of microscopic creatures. Yet here, inside this flimsy cocoon, hurtling through space at over seventeen thousand miles an hour, he had been able to take his time and methodically retrieve every last vital drop, even those no bigger than pinheads.

Josh stopped exercising and knelt by his bunk.

"Thank you, Lord. Thy will be done on Earth, just as it has been done today in your heavens. For You are the Power, the Truth and the Provider. And will be forever and ever. Amen."

****

LENDING A HAND

Hayley stood in the doorway of the cabin, watching her parents stumble through the pine trees to their car. They had their backs to her, but she could tell they were still going at it hammer and tongs.

Mom didn't want her to stay here on her own, not even for a few days. She said it was way too soon after the accident. For heaven's sake, there were wild animals in this neck of the woods – bobcats even – and who *knew* what could happen?

Dad was every bit as concerned as Mom, but he respected Hayley's decision not to have a prosthesis. When Seth, one of the occupational therapists, offered the use of his cabin in the mountains overlooking San Jose, Dad suggested to Hayley that here was an ideal opportunity to learn how to cope with everyday tasks without Mom or him butting in, trying to help. He made a tool belt with pockets for a phone; a rug-making hook; a small, sharp pair of scissors; a slim flashlight; and a big pocket for whatever else she might need. Then he attached the tools to the belt with stretchy strings so that the equipment could be tucked into the pockets. He insisted that Hayley wear the belt, all day and every day.

And that was how she came to be standing in the doorway of the cabin, her bandaged stump held against her waist, sensing fingers that no longer existed. She raised her right hand hesitantly to eye level when her parents reached the road and turned to wave goodbye.

She was alone to cope with whatever the next six days threw at her. Mom and Dad promised to call at eight o'clock every night, to check on her and make sure she was okay.

After arranging her few clothes in the bureau, she decided to put up her new poster of her idol, Bethany Hamilton who exultantly rode the waves. *Losing a hand is small potatoes to having an arm amputated*, Hayley thought.

She found the cardboard tube, held it between her feet and knees, and pulled off the cap. The poster coiled snugly inside the tube and refused to budge when she pinched it between finger and thumb. She thought for a moment, and then decided – no problem! She could use the hook. She dug the point in about an inch from the poster's edge and eased the precious picture a few inches out of the tube before she tugged the poster the rest of the way out.

It sprang apart in her hand, like a pack of ready-to-bake biscuits. The suddenness startled her and she dropped it. She picked it up and rolled it out on the table, but as soon as one end lay flat, the other coiled, so she flipped it over and tried to roll it the other way. Without thinking, she smoothed the back with her stump and winced. It was too soon to use it.

The poster rolled off the table and bounced onto the rug, giving Hayley an idea. She collected the four books she'd brought to help pass the time, and knelt beside the poster. Then she placed a book on each corner while she unraveled the slippery paper so that it lay, face down, on the rug. That accomplished, she jumped up and down, backwards and forwards, until the poster had been flattened, ready to submit to her will.

Haha! Now I'm motoring, she thought.

Maybe not. Mom and Dad brought everything she could possibly need, except thumb tacks and tape. Hayley looked around for something sticky. She had plenty of *Orbit* in her bag, and her jaws ached by the time she'd chewed eight pieces to the right consistency. She put the blobs on the back of the poster. Then, using her forehead to hold the poster in place, she pressed on the gum and fixed it to the wall.

The poster wasn't straight, but it was up. She did a little dance.

Throughout the next day, Sunday, the weather was iffy, and she watched *The Lion King* twice while still in her pajamas, before spending the next two hours on her phone, catching up with school friends.

"Hales! How you doing, girl?" Brittany asked, before professing undying love for Dave, same as she had for Steve, before the accident. "Scott was asking after you," she added.

Scott was Brittany's nerdy brother, and she'd been trying to set up a date between him and Hayley for months.

"Say hi to him," Hayley said. "Hey, how are you doing with that fool science project?"

At six o'clock, she realized she had nothing to brag about. Yesterday, Mom and Dad had been impressed by her poster-mounting achievement.

She was hungry and decided to make pancakes. Seth had left a bag of flour in his dry goods cupboard, and she had plenty of eggs. The glass bowl skidded over the table while she stirred the batter until she trapped it between the books. *Good idea bringing them.*

Then the handle of the pan got so hot that she had to use a dish towel to hold it, but she didn't see the dangling corner until it caught fire. In a panic she beat the towel on the edge of the sink while the cabin filled with smoke and her pancake burned. She ate it anyway and didn't mention the fire when Mom called. She would've been there in a heartbeat, taking over.

The sun came out on Monday. It glinted on the new grass sprouting along the path and revealed dust motes floating in the cabin. Hayley strolled outside in her bare feet, and breathed in the sharp, pine-scented air while she gazed at the blue, blue sky swathing the purple hills over the eastern side of the valley. Buds on the rhododendron by the door had opened, revealing pink flowers. Dutch crocuses and irises peeped through the soil under the windows, and lupins competed with daylilies around the small square of grass in front of the cabin.

It was a glorious spring day – an artist's day.

After breakfast, she washed the dingy windows, swept the cabin floor, dusted and polished until the air inside the cabin rivaled the freshness outside. Her energy seemed boundless. She went outside and pulled up clumps of rough grass to give the flowering plants growing room. It took her all morning and more than a couple of hours after lunch.

Only then did tiredness hit her. She had to stop. It wouldn't do to fall into the trap she'd been warned about – doing too much with her good limb and hurting that. She went inside, gave Bethany a high five, and curled up in a chair with *Walk Two Moons* for the rest of the afternoon.

Tuesday came blessed with bright sunshine, too. She put on shorts, a sleeveless top, her sneakers with the curly laces that she didn't have to tie, and went outside to exercise. After running on the spot, she started practising her cheerleading routine and tumbled into an awkward, one-handed cartwheel.

While sitting on the grass, she nibbled her thumb nail.

Okay, I can't do cartwheels yet, but what about flips?

She jumped up and, with her heart thudding, ran from one edge of the grass to the other, tossing herself head over heels in the process, and landed neatly on both feet. Then she tried a back flip, and did it perfectly. Laughing like a clown, she flung herself backwards and forwards until she collapsed on the grass, out of breath but with enough energy to create angel shapes in the grass.

Yay! Yay! She could still be on the team!

She ran indoors, gave Bethany a smack of a high-five, grabbed her phone and punched coach Fran Pascoe's number, dancing on the spot, humming, while she waited to connect.

"Hales, sweetheart!" Fran said, as soon as she realized who was calling. "We've missed you big time. The team's not the same without you. What are you up to these days?"

"I'm on a week's vacation. Fran, I gotta tell you. I can still do the jumps. Honest to God, I can. Gotta work on the cartwheels, but I'm good with the jumps and my feet and shoulders are fine. I can still be in the pyramid."

No sound came from the other end of the line.

"Fran? Fran? You still there?"

"Yeah, I'm here. Um, Hales, it sounds as if ... silly me, you can't be ... ."

"Can't be what?"

"Expecting to make the team again."

"But I can! I can do the jumps, and---"

Fran butted in. "You've only got one hand, sweetheart."

"So?"

"So you can only shake one pompom. It would spoil the routine. Besides," Fran hesitated before adding, "besides we've filled your place. Had to, honey. You do understand, don't you?"

Hayley's excitement vanished. She heard herself say, "Sure, Fran. Sure."

"I'm real sorry, Hales. Now you take good care. 'Bye, sweetheart."

She felt flat and drained. She sank onto the bed and depression threatened to swamp her. With an effort, she shook it off, but she couldn't stem her anger.

"Why me? Why me?" she shouted. "Why not him? He's gotten off scot free. But me? Me? I'll **never** be the same. **Not ever**."

Memory came unbidden and she relived the day when she'd been standing on Brittany's driveway, waiting for her friend to collect whatever it was she'd forgotten before they went to town. Brittany was skipping down the porch steps when Steve came roaring up the drive on his Harley, showing off, throwing wheelies, skidding on the gravel and scaring Hayley half to death while she dodged away from the huge machine each time he deliberately aimed it at her.

"Catch you next time," he shouted, when she leapt into the flowerbed.

And he had.

Half-way down the drive, he turned too sharply and lost control. He fell off the bike and landed flat on his back. Without a rider, the Harley zoomed towards Hayley who was looking at the plant she had crushed. Too late, she saw the bike coming and tried to avoid it, but she stumbled and fell, arms thrown wide, onto the drive.

The Harley crashed into the stone border of the flowerbed and toppled onto its side. The spinning back wheel jerked and bounced on her left hand, grinding it into the gravel, until the engine cut out and her hand took the full weight of the smoking back tire.

The raw grazes on Hayley's face eventually healed, but her hand was beyond saving.

Brittany broke up with Steve there and then. Other than that, he lost nothing. His Harley was soon repaired and there were no legal repercussions, his insurers insisting that the incident had taken place on private property.

"You're not going to sue me. Say you're not going to sue me," Steve pleaded. "I didn't set out to hurt you. You know I didn't."

Hayley threw herself onto the bed and cried, until, exhausted, she fell asleep, her right hand on the wet pillow.

When she woke, it was mid-afternoon and her stomach gurgled, reminding her she'd had nothing to eat all day. She scolded herself while warming soup in the microwave. Common sense should have told her Fran wouldn't put her back on the team where she could jeopardize them all. On the other hand, her heart told her it was only natural to be upset. Hadn't she just found something she could still do well, where having one hand didn't seem to matter?

"There'll be other things, won't there, Bethany?" she asked the crooked poster. "I'll find something else."

When Mom and Dad called, she told them about her conversation with Fran.

Mom said, "Honey, what did you expect? It stands to reason you couldn't go back on it."

Dad said, "What about soccer, Hayley? I bet you'd be good at that."

She said she would think about it.

Wednesday morning dawned cool and cloudy and Hayley decided to carry on writing a story about a sixteen-year-old star point guard of a girls' basketball team. She'd started typing it on her laptop, but after the accident she bought a notebook, into which she pasted a printed version of what she had written so far. Without intending to, she found herself editing what she had written so enthusiastically, now uncertain about tense and POV. By lunchtime, she hadn't added anything new, and she was completely fed up.

The sun broke through the clouds and its beams came through the freshly-washed windows, brightening the cabin and adding sparkles to the mugs and plates displayed on the Welsh dresser. She pulled on a sweatshirt and decided to go for a walk. Perhaps inspiration would come while she rambled through the trees.

It was peaceful in the shadowy, green forest. She watched insects flit above the ferns through stray sunbeams, wings momentarily gilded before winking out. At first, all she heard was her own breathing, but gradually she became aware of other noises around her. The undergrowth rustled, and a pair of dark-coated coyotes sniffed their way through the tangle. They stopped, one dainty foot raised, and she kept absolutely still until they moved silently on.

The quiet was shattered when something crashed in the undergrowth not far away. Three deer fled past her, but the noise continued. She crept forward and found a young doe thrashing and kicking, trying to free herself of a thin white cord that wound round her back legs. On seeing Hayley, the doe tried to spring away, but she tumbled onto her side, and blood spurted from a cut caused by the restricting cord. Again and again, she tried to stand, to crash into the ferns, panting, eyes rolling.

Hayley pulled the flashlight out of her tool belt and, while the doe still lay on the ground, shone its beam into the animal's eyes. The doe froze.

Hayley inched nearer until she could reach the creature's legs. Then she gripped the flashlight between her teeth and fumbled for her scissors. She established where the thread cut most deeply into the leg, and snipped it. The doe went to spring away, but Hayley put down the scissors and laid her hand on the heaving grayish-brown coat. She was ready to scramble away if the deer threatened to bite her, but the animal lay still.

With scissors in hand again, Hayley cut another thread, another, and another, removing strands as she did so. Saliva dripped from her mouth while she tried to hold the flashlight steady. Her tongue felt coated with metal, and her teeth ached.

Then the doe found she was free. She moved her legs and bent to lick the cuts. She lifted her head and touched the back of Hayley's hand, as if to thank her. Then, with a twitch of her big ears, she was up and away, and was soon out of sight.

Hayley stowed the pieces of cord in her big pocket, and combed the ferns with her fingers, seeking more. She found a long silky string – a kite string – which led her to a clearing that abutted the road. At some time during the fall, a family had camped there. They had left their trash behind in a black plastic bag, now torn to shreds by inquisitive animals.

What a mess! Litter strewed the ground. The plastic core around which the kite string had been wound lay beneath one of the trees. Hayley put that in her pocket, too, and retraced her steps to where she had freed the deer. Nearby, she found a broken kite lodged in the branches of a pine tree.

When her parents called that evening, she kept quiet about the deer, but did tell them about the kite and the mess in the clearing.

They told her not to tackle it on her own: they would bring trash bags with them and help her clean up before taking her home on Friday.

It rained heavily on Thursday and Hayley was content to stay indoors. She turned her notebook around and started scribbling a story about a herd of deer whose habitat was lost when developers moved in. Now and then she stopped writing to snack on chips and soda. Suddenly it was dark. She had written twenty pages. Time to stop for dinner.

Mom and Dad cleaned up the camping area on Friday morning. Hayley was content to follow them, dragging a plastic bag behind her while they dumped trash in it. Soon it was time to lock up the cabin and head for home, and then to the clinic to have her dressing changed. She thanked Seth for letting her stay at the cabin, and told him about the trash.

"Some people!" he sighed. "You should see the mess in the Guadalupe right now. Some of us are organizing a clean-up on April 30th. Do you want to give us a hand?"

"Will they let me?"

"Sure. Why not?"

Seth wrote down the URL of a web page which gave all the details and Hayley checked it out when she went home. There were over two dozen distressing photographs illustrating the trash suffocating the river. Seeing them made Hayley all the more determined to do her bit, and, on Saturday morning, two weeks later, Mom dropped her off outside Target in Coleman Avenue and told her to call when she wanted to come home.

It was a short walk to New Autumn Street, and Hayley soon found the center of operations for the clean-up. There she was directed to a room off to the right, where she found herself at the back of a crowd of people. In a corner, a plump woman whose name tag identified her as Helen handed out bottles of water.

Hayley dodged through the crowd. "Is this where I sign up?" she asked. "I've come to give a hand."

Helen stopped what she was doing. She eyed Hayley's bandaged stump, and then came to bend protectively over her, the way Mom always did when delivering bad news. She patted Hayley's shoulder.

Tears spiked Hayley's eye lashes as she told herself "She's not going to let me. I've come all this way for nothing."

"You're way too generous, honey," Helen said. "You don't have to give us a hand, but we'd sure like to borrow one."

She grinned and Hayley couldn't help smiling back.

"Come over here, honey," Helen went on, "and collect your water and trash bags. I sure wish there were more people like you in the world today."

****

AN ACT OF GOD

The chattering television blinked and fell silent. Every other electrical appliance in the house also stopped working and darkness, heavy as a winter blanket, covered Eileen.

She dropped her knitting, clutched the collar of her shirt with both hands, and listened.

Now that she couldn't hear the game show, the settling sounds of the old farmhouse unnerved her: spooky, creaking, rustling sounds. They scared her, but not as much as the dark. She was petrified of the dark.

She bit her nails as she tried to remember where Ben kept his flashlight. Huge and heavy, it had a beam that seemed to stretch for miles. It was probably under the kitchen sink. She groped her way through the now unfamiliar house. On reaching the kitchen door, she opened it a fraction. Stopped. Listened. Mice scampered across the floor. She was scared of mice.

She closed the door again and leaned her forehead on it. She felt it shake in the draught. Under her feet, the floorboards shook, too, as the old house fought against the gale that roared around it like a hungry beast, tearing off shingles and slamming shutters. Thuds and crashes outside overrode the creaks and groans inside. She wished Ben was home. He should've been home by now. Where *was* he?

Eileen turned, rested her back on the door, and mentally searched rooms, trying to locate another battery-powered light. There was Casey's night light. It wasn't very big, but it was better than nothing. She ought to bring her little boy downstairs anyway, before the storm woke him and he started crying. She had to be brave for him.

By trailing her fingers along the wall, she found her way to the stairs. Her hand touched the coiled telephone wire and her heart leaped. Maybe it still worked.

Please, please make it work.

She lifted the receiver and listened. No dialing tone. She and Casey were trapped in this cold dark place, miles from anywhere or anyone. Their home lay in the crook of a right-angled bend on a lonely road. Chuck and Lorna Stallebrass, their nearest neighbors, lived five miles down the stretch of road that led south. Eastbound, the road ambled on for twenty miles before it finally reached a gas station.

BANG! BANG! Crash! Bang! Clatter, clatter, rumble, rumble, rumblerumblerumble.

The hullabaloo came from the kitchen. On legs that threatened to give way, Eileen retraced her steps. The kitchen door wouldn't open. With arms extended, she strained to push it until she made a gap just wide enough to squeeze through. Once in the kitchen, she had to move quickly sideways to avoid being hit by the door. It slammed shut again, and the latch grazed her arm.

The heavy old back door stood wide open, its catch torn out of the frame. An icy wind whistled around the kitchen, dashing cups, plates, utensils – anything it could grab – onto the floor. Near Eileen, the round trash barrel had blown in from the yard. It spun against the wall, tumbling the remaining trash inside it.

With her hair and clothes blowing every which way, Eileen leaned into the wind and struggled to reach the back door. Through its gaping frame she saw shredded black clouds race across a frowning moon. A huge pine tree, barely thirty feet away, rocked in the gale.

Grit, pine needles and twigs blew into the kitchen, adding to the mess. She gave up the fight and clung to the edge of the sink, unable to win any more ground.

She didn't hear the car pull up, wasn't aware of the bulky figure creeping along the side of the house, head bent into the wind, until he stood on the doorstep. His right side, the side nearest to the drive, was edged with reflected light from the car's headlamps. The rest of him was in shadow. Eileen couldn't see his face.

She screamed and staggered back, her heart pounding.

The man stepped into the kitchen and seemed to melt into the wall. The view of the yard diminished, and with it, the wind. She realised he was pushing the door shut. Darkness was complete, but from the sounds coming from the doorway, he was sliding the top bolt into place. Then he kicked the bottom one home.

The trash barrel stopped trundling. The slats of the blind stopped rattling. The wind raged outside, but in the kitchen it was still and quiet and dark. Very dark.

The man came towards Eileen, breathing heavily.

Who was he? "D-don't hurt me. P-please don't hurt me," she pleaded.

"Jeez, honey. Me hurt you? What the heck you a-thinkin' of?"

She recognised his voice. "Chuck?"

"Sure is, honey."

"I'm sorry. I didn't recognize you. Oh, Chuck, I'm so scared."

"Ben said you'd like as not be a-pooping your pants."

"You've heard from Ben? What's happened to him? Where is he?"

"Sweatin' it out at the office. Th'whole intire eastern seaboard's shut down. He called me. Asked me to stop by and see you're okay. Which you definitely ain't."

"W-we'll be all right. We've got blankets and some bottled water---"

Chuck interrupted her. "Now you listen to me, honey. I seen that big ol' pine a-whippin' about there out back, a-bending more'n

129

my pole a-playing a wily ol' striped bass. An' you with a broken door, an' all. It ain't safe to be a-staying here. Now, you run an' git that boy of yourn while I see what vittals I kin salvage. Ain't you got no candles?"

"Ben's flashlight's under the sink."

"Git goin', honey."

Eileen hurried upstairs.

Ten minutes later she was helping a well-wrapped Casey climb into the back of the car, while Chuck stowed plastic bags of perishables in the trunk. Then, drowning the wail of the wind, they heard a wrenching, grinding, tearing sound. It came from the back yard.

"Git in! Git in!"

Chuck slammed the car door, almost trapping her foot. He hauled himself round the car, hand over hand, and tumbled into the driver's seat where the engine chugged noisily. He slammed the lever into reverse and rammed the gas pedal to the floor.

With a snarl, the car flew backwards, fishtailing from verge to verge, while a black giant with multiple flailing arms sprang towards them over the roof of the house.

The car was still speeding backwards when a deafening crash shook the ground. The car leapt into the air. It landed heavily, jarring every bone in their bodies. Eileen found herself sprawled over Casey. She crawled off him and hugged him to her. He buried his face in her coat and clung to her.

She peered through the space between the front seats. Chuck's face was buried in the wheel and his hands dangled. Bits of twig flew past the windows but she heard nothing, nothing but a strange sighing. She let go of Casey and popped her ears. Then she heard debris raining on the roof.

The engine had died. Chuck straightened up, wiped his face, and turned the key. He was obviously relieved when, after a few splutters, the engine brummed into life again. He waited until it was idling evenly before he switched on the headlamps and their beams cut into the darkness. Directly in front of them, the black monster pinned its prey. They watched, horrified, as it settled lower and lower, breaking the backbone of her home.

Chuck dabbed blood off his face and asked, "You insured?"

"Yes." It came out as a squeak.

"Against Acts of God?"

Eileen cleared her throat. "That wasn't an Act of God."

"Insurers will say it was."

"No, Chuck, it wasn't. Now, you coming to fetch us ... *that* was an Act of God."

****

PAINTING THE TOWN RED

"The gang's coming at 7.30 to pick me up. Then we're going out to paint the town red."

"Oh, no, you're not, young lady."

Emma turned, surprise and sudden anger flushing her cheeks. "But it's our graduation party. Why can't I have a good time like everyone else?"

"I didn't say you couldn't." Dad lowered his paper and patted the arm of his overstuffed chair, inviting his daughter to come sit there.

Emma plumped down beside him. "So what's the difference between painting the town red and having a good time?"

"You really don't know?"

"I thought they meant the same thing. But you're going to put me right, aren't you?"

"Yes, I am. Now, are you sitting comfortably? I'm going to tell you a story."

Emma sighed and rolled her eyes, but she leaned back against the wing of the chair and rested her hands in her lap.

--o--

Once upon a time, in 1837, to be exact, in a beautiful English town called Melton Mowbray, where they make the most scrumptious pies, there lived an immensely rich man and his not quite so rich but definitely very wealthy companions.

The rich man was the Third Marquess of Waterford. Waterford is a place in Ireland. Now don't ask me why an Irish peer should live in the middle of England, because I don't know. However, I do know that, at twenty-six years of age, he was definitely old enough to know right from wrong, and so were his friends.

Lord Waterford was commonly known as "the Mad Marquis". By drinking, fighting, stealing, vandalizing property, and hunting a poor parson with bloodhounds, Lord Waterford brought shame on his noble family.

That day in 1837, after a successful fox hunt, the drunken Mad Marquis and his hooligan friends ran riot in Melton Mowbray. They found several cans of red paint and daubed it on the town's toll booth, post office and other buildings in the High Street. The *White Swan* quickly became the *Red Swan*.

Not content with defacing property, the yobboes (for that is what we'd call them now) assaulted innocent civilians. They knocked down a constable, the town jailor, and a night watchman and smothered them with red paint. They tried to overturn a caravan in which a man was sleeping. He would have been killed if they'd been successful. Then they broke into the jail and released a prisoner.

What was the outcome of this outrageous spree?

In July, 1838, Lord Waterford and his companions were charged with rioting, but were acquitted and convicted only of common assault. Had these hooligans been of humble birth they would have been jailed and sentenced to hard labor, but remember I told you they were very wealthy. The fine imposed upon each of them (£100) presented no hardship. One hundred pounds then would be worth about three thousand pounds today, but such was Lord Waterford's wealth that fining him one hundred pounds was tantamount to fining a workman sixpence then.

It was a typical case of one law for the rich and another for the poor.

It was this incident that reputedly brought a new phrase into the English language, that of "painting the town red". The meaning has changed somewhat over the years but it still means indulging in unrestrained – usually drunken – activity.

--o--

Emma's father sneaked an arm around his daughter's waist and pulled her onto his knee. "Have you been listening to anything I've said?"

"Yes, Dad. Every word."

"So what are you going to do tonight?"

"I'm going to have a good time, but I won't make you ashamed of me."

"That's my girl. Now you'd better go and get ready. Your friends will be here soon."

****

LOWEST EARTH ORBIT

Duncan's thick socks slid down again, exposing his painfully thin legs to the frosty air, while he ran towards the noisy group of children that jostled and sparred around two teachers. His mother plodded after him.

A boy on the edge of the crowd called, "Dunk! Are ye comin'?"

"Nae, Gordy. I wish."

Miss Killwarden stopped counting heads, her finger poised over a girl's hoodie. She smiled sadly at Duncan's mother. "'Tis a shame he canna come, Annie. If he were just a mite bigger. No so wee..."

"He'll catch up one day. He's comin' wi' me ter work ter learn how we make satellites."

"Ye'll like that, Duncan. Write an essay and read it in class on Monday."

"The bus is coming, Miss!"

Gordy pointed down Houldsworth Street at a minibus whose windows and fittings sparkled in the cold sun. As it drew near, Duncan squinted to read its destination: British Interplanetary Society. LONDON.

"Line up everyone, and pick up your stuff," called Miss Killwarden. "If you need the toilet, go now. McDonalds said ye can use theirs. 'Tis a long ride to London."

Duncan tugged Gordy's arm. "Dinna forget ye promised to bring me summat from the exhibition."

He stepped back and stood beside Annie, either yanking up his socks or thumping the tops of his arms to keep warm, while his friends boarded.

When the bus pulled away, the driver pipped his horn, Gordy banged on the window, and Duncan waved until the bus rounded a corner and went out of sight.

135

--o--

Iain stuck his head inside the canteen door. "Has your lad finished his snack?" he asked Annie.

"Aye."

"Bring your things, laddie. Ye'll be with me 'til four o'clock."

"Are ye sure, Mr. Thomson? He'll be fine wi' me. He's got a book."

"It's up to ye, Duncan. Ye can sit next to yer ma and read, or come and talk to me. Ye can sit in my big chair. It swivels just fine."

"Cor! Can I?"

Iain smiled at Annie. "Pick him up from my office after ye clock off."

"Thank you, Mr. Thomson."

Duncan looked lost in the huge chair. After swiveling to and fro – he hadn't the power or the room to make it turn full circle – he stretched over the polished desk and tried to reach the perpetual motion balls.

Iain hitched the straight-backed chair nearer to the front of his desk. It was an unfamiliar position for him. "Tell me, laddie," he said, "what do ye know about communication satellites?"

"Sir Arthur Clarke first thought them up. He got a medal for it. He would've been a hundred tomorrer if he hadn't died. 'Tis my birthday tomorrer an' I'll be ten."

"Is it now? And what will ye be doing on your birthday?"

"I wanted ter go ter the big do at the British Interplan...plan... summat Society, 'cause I'm a member, but I haveta take medicines, an' the teachers can't be doing wi' that, not fer three days straight, so I can't."

"That's a shame."

"Aye. But Ma's throwin' a party fer me ter make up fer it."

Duncan suddenly slid off the swivel chair and stood by the desk. Iain could see nothing of him except his fingers gripping the edge, and his head, from the eyes up. "Can I draw?" he asked.

"Er, aye. Of course. Use my blotter. Pencils are in the top drawer."

The boy clambered back onto the big chair, knelt in it, and tried to bump it nearer the desk.

"No having much success there, are ye, laddie? Let's swap seats."

Iain took his rightful place behind the desk while Duncan scampered round to the front. He tugged the interviewee's chair into position, and knelt on it. Then Iain pushed the blotter over.

"Got my own pencil," the boy said, while fishing in his trouser pocket.

He spread his arms over the blotter. His tongue flickered while the blunt pencil etched thick lines into the soft white paper.

Iain watched the drawing take shape. "What is it?"

"A communications satellite."

"It looks like a box kite to me."

"I haven't drawn the bit what holds the message yet."

"What are ye going to use for that? And how will ye launch it?"

"Dunno. But I'll think of summat."

--o--

The shopkeeper handed over the helium-filled balloon to Duncan's dad. "Happy birthday," he said to Duncan. "And how old are ye the day?"

"Ten."

"Really? I'd've put ye at eight. What've ye got there?"

"'Tis a communications satellite. Made it myself."

"Looks like a box kite to me."

Duncan sighed. "Ev'rybody says that."

The shopkeeper leaned over. "How does it work?"

"We haveta squish the frame into a diamond and push the balloon inside. There. Jus' like that. Can ye tie a loop in the string, Da, real near the balloon? That's it. Then these strings on the frame go through the loop an' we tie 'em all together."

"Where's your message, son?"

"Here."

Duncan pulled the crumpled luggage label out of his pocket, threaded it onto one of the strings, and knotted them again.

"Let's go see if it works, Da."

"Hold tight to yon balloon, laddie. 'Tis braw windy the day. Ye dinna want it to blow awa'."

They were crossing the street when a gust of wind hit them so hard it felt like a punch in the back. Another gust buffeted them, another, and another. The last one made Dad stumble, and it lifted Duncan clear off his feet.

Up, up it blew him, with Duncan clinging onto the balloon string.

Higher and higher.

Dad raced below, leaping, trying to reach the weight at the end of the string, impossibly high above him.

The wind blew Duncan toward a towering horse chestnut tree and he crashed into it. The string of the balloon tangled in the branches, leaving Duncan suspended twenty feet above the ground.

Dad came pounding below the tree just as the string ripped itself out of his terrified son's hands. The home-made satellite soared into the sky.

138

In a cascade of leaves and small twigs, Duncan plummeted to earth.

"I've got ye! I've got ye!"

Dad wrapped his arms around Duncan's legs, pulled the boy to him and was knocked to the ground. The force of the impact left both of them breathless and trembling. For long minutes, neither had the strength to sit up.

Then Duncan pointed at a golden box in the sky. "Look at it go, Da! Look at it go!" he shouted. "It works. My satellite works. Who do ye think will get my message?"

"Someone in Africa, at the rate it's travelling. But as long as it's no you a-flying through the sky, I dinna care."

Duncan giggled. "I was in low earth orbit for a bit there, wasn't I, Da?"

"Ye could put it like that."

"Can I tell Gordy? He'll be that jealous."

"If ye want to. But no a word to your Ma, mind. Come on, let's away to your party, and gie ye some ballast."

****

A CULTURAL EXCHANGE

That night, in July, 1947, Josh had made camp on the lower slopes of Jicarilla Peak. It was late, too late to read any more, and he put down his dog-eared copy of the Journal of the British Interplanetary Society, sent to him by his friend in England. Sid was just as mad about space exploration as he was, and they swapped literature. Josh stared at the stars, and wondered whether it would ever be possible to reach them.

The wind picked up and a summer storm started. Lightning zipped across the scrub brush, each spasm etching the stark scene into his brain. Thunder boomed loud on the heels of the blinding flashes. It didn't scare Josh. He'd seen many similar storms in the New Mexico desert, but this one was unique in its intensity. He watched its glory while lying on his belly, peeping through the flap of his tent.

Another blistering shaft of lightning tore the sky apart. It was followed by a thunder crash, directly overhead. Josh flinched. Fat, slow drops of rain plopped onto his tent and he reached to close the flap when he saw a glowing triangular object streak north across the sky and vanish into an arroyo. A second later a white-hot ball of fire burst from the gully. Heat or steam from the spot caused the hills behind it to shimmer as if they were a mirage. Lightning flashed again, but it was pale by comparison with the eye-searing explosion, and he hardly heard the ensuing thunder.

A plane must have been brought down by the storm, Josh thought, and he wondered what he could do. From his position there was little he **could** do, but the small towns of Ramona and Mesa were quite near the gully. They must have seen the crash and would send out a rescue team. He wriggled out of his tent and, slipping and sliding, scrambled down to a ridge above a level stretch of ground, where he stared east across the desert, looking for headlights.

The air around him vibrated, as if agitated by a powerful engine. Josh looked up to see a glowing object, similar to the one that had crashed, disappear behind the mountain.

*What was **that**?*

If it was a plane, he'd never seen anything like it before.

The air vibrated again, stronger this time, making Josh's stomach churn. The sensation eased and he looked around. A sleek, delta-shaped object had landed on the plateau, barely two hundred yards away. It glowed eerily in the dark.

Josh's heart leapt. For years he had longed to spot a UFO and now – unless he was dreaming – he was looking right at one. It couldn't be anything else.

He climbed back to his tent, looking frequently over his shoulder to make sure the craft was still there, grabbed his notebook and box camera, and then skidded down the slope back to the plateau. He came to a halt when he was within fifty feet of the spaceship.

A band of light streamed through an opening in the side nearest to him while a ramp slowly emerged below the gap. Silhouetted against the light, he saw two figures. Their heads were disproportionately large for their short, skinny bodies. If it hadn't been for the oversized heads, they could have been mistaken for undernourished children.

Josh lifted the camera and focused on the pair.

Click. Got it!

The aliens walked down the ramp, scanning left and right with enormous dark eyes. One looked his way and, as its glance fell on him, Josh felt as if he were a metal object being drawn to a magnet. Against his will, he crept towards the ship until he stood in front of the creatures. They approached him. Each of them took one of his hands and, walking backwards, they tugged him up the ramp.

As he neared the portal, a thought flashed through Josh's mind.

The aliens are outside their ship, apparently breathing normally. If they can breathe Earth's air, I can breathe theirs. I wonder what else our worlds have in common.

While the portal closed behind him, Josh realized he was eager to find out.

--o--

It was daylight when they landed, and Josh woke to find himself strapped into a bunk with the alien crew standing near him. He expected to be interrogated, but all they did was to untie the bunk straps. Then one helped him to sit up, while another brought him a beaker of thick green liquid.

"Dr-r-ink. You m-u-ust dr-r-ink," the alien said. He sounded like a run-down gramophone.

He placed the beaker on a shelf near Josh's bunk, and then both of them left, leaving the door wide open behind them.

Josh took it to be an invitation to follow them if he wanted to. He stumbled to the portal and looked out. The ramp was down. There was nothing to stop him leaving the ship. Nothing – except the fear of what lay outside.

He was thirsty and eyed the liquid for a long time, but then he decided they wouldn't have brought him all this way to poison him, so he took a sip. It tasted good and he drank it slowly.

When dusk fell, two different aliens came into the ship. They exchanged the empty beaker for a full one, before taking one of his arms each and leading him to the portal. They let go of him. One of them pressed a button and the portal closed. He lifted Josh's hand, forced one of his fingers onto the same button, made Josh press it, and the door slid open again. Josh watched, puzzled, when they started walking down the ramp.

"Hey! What's going on? What do I do now?" he called from the open doorway.

They returned to the top of the ramp. "This your house. This where you live," one said.

Josh's eyes popped. "Really?" was all he could say.

The other one told him, "We give you a home. You live here until we need ship again."

Josh could hardly believe his luck. He soon adapted to his new quarters and spent hours amusing himself on the flight deck, captain of his own starship. Gradually, the feeling of being a captive faded, for the aliens allowed him to roam at will almost anywhere.

The days were longer and colder than they were on Earth. After each day ticked away on his Concord wristwatch (a coming-of-age present from his parents), Josh made a mark in his notebook. In time the pencil wore away, but the aliens gave him a black rod which lasted years.

He missed the pleasure of biting and chewing food, for the aliens only drank a mixture of blended vegetables and fruit juice. They didn't wear clothes, either, even on the coldest days. Their dark skin was as thick and tough as elephant hide. Josh became used to the climate and walked around naked during the warmer seasons. He cut vines into lengths and flogged them against stones, and then wove the softened threads into a poncho that he wore when the temperature dropped.

The aliens' children were inquisitive and not at all afraid of him. They tugged his fingers, toes and ears, and pushed their skinny fingers up his nostrils. They had tiny noses and their mouths were small slits. After they tired of examining him, they hung on his back like monkeys, played with his beard, or fought for turns to sit on his knee.

One of the children became special to Josh. They didn't appear to have names, so he called them by letters of the alphabet, and this one he called Deebee. During one harsh winter, Josh wore two ponchos. Deebee, then tiny, smaller and thinner than any of the others, crouched in a corner of the schoolroom, while his friends leapt and ran around, ignoring him. Josh walked over to him, sat down, drew the waif onto his crossed legs, and wrapped the ponchos around both of them. Gradually Josh's body warmth seeped into Deebee's cold limbs, and the child fell asleep. Josh was nodding, too, until an adult came and held out her arms, as if to take Deebee.

Josh tightened his hold, and challenged her with his eyes.

She stared back, puzzled. "It is his end time," she said. "I will put him on the end stone for the birds."

After Josh protested, she left them alone. For the next two days, Deebee slept in the ship with Josh, and sat on his knee under the poncho while listening in the schoolroom. On the third day, however, he joined the rest of the class, as lively and mischievous as they were.

In an attempt to learn about their way of life, Josh joined in the children's lessons. It was hard and frustrating, but gradually he mastered their language. By that means he found out that his new home lay in the center of a brilliant globular cluster, thirty-four thousand light years from Earth. He struggled to remember his astronomy and guessed that the star he was on lay in the middle of Messier 3.

But then he had doubts. The journey from Earth had taken an impossibly short time for such a distance, and he asked for an explanation. While using an interactive diagram of Space, the starship crew showed him that, every so often, a wormhole appeared, creating a short cut.

"Can I go home the next time it comes round?" he asked.

"Why? You have everything you need, and the children love you."

"But I don't belong here," he said, spreading his hands.

After a long silence, the captain said, "If we take you, will you bring a friend back with you?"

Josh hesitated before saying he would. He had no intention of leaving Earth a second time. Then he asked, "How long do I have to wait?"

They told him that the wormhole had been in the right place two years ago, and the next opportunity would not present itself until 2013 – another twenty Earth years. Josh caught his breath. By then he would be eighty-seven, an old man. Assuming he was still alive, he might not be strong enough to make the journey.

While waiting, he taught the children about Earth, its lands, climate and oceans, and as much history as he could remember. He also made sketches of the aliens' oddly-shaped houses, birds and wild animals. The drawings looked nothing like the originals to begin with, but his artistry improved as time went on. He also collected leaves from the plants in the wilderness outside the ship and pasted them into his notebook.

The years crept by until, finally, the wormhole was in the right place, and Josh looked forward to returning to Earth. He looked on anxiously while the aliens checked the shell and controls of the spaceship, and heaved a sigh of relief when they pronounced it fit to use.

He couldn't believe it was really happening. After sixty-six years, he was going home, and, given the speed that the starship was traveling, they should cover the remaining distance in seven Earth days. Deebee and Seezee stood at the controls, while the relief crew, Exgee and Ayjay slept.

Deebee came over to Josh's bunk. "You must strap in," he said. "Soon we go through the solar wind skin."

Josh scratched his beard. "Solar wind skin? Oh, you must mean the heliosheath. Are we really as near to Earth as that?"

"Yes. And it is very dangerous just inside the skin. All things must be secured. Robots will steer the ship until we are through the magnetic bubbles."

The starship tipped to an angle of forty-five degrees and Josh felt a tremor as the craft pierced the heliosheath. The ship bounced and jerked, as if it were on the surface of boiling liquid before it leveled out and their passage was smoother, with occasional jolts.

Deebee and Seezee unstrapped their restrainers and went forward to the flight deck where they scanned a star-strewn screen. Seezee pointed to a white dot and they argued heatedly until Deebee ran to Josh's bunk.

"Come. See."

"What is it?"

Seezee pointed at the dot which lay some way ahead. As the ship zoomed towards it, and its shape became clearer, Josh decided it was man-made. Its main feature was a large white dish that had a spear protruding from its center. A jumble of metal boxes lay around and behind the dish, and a long metal arm probed space in front.

"Is it from your world?" Deebee asked.

"Got to be. Can you get closer so I can have a better look?"

Seezee pulled on a white, thick suit that he'd taken from a compartment in the flight deck and moved into the airlock, while Deebee roused the relief crew to get their help.

Within seconds the starship was bobbing beside the object. Deebee pressed a button on the control panel, after which Josh saw Seezee shoot into space, trailing a tether. He was tossed around, but finally succeeded in hooking the tether onto one of the struts below the dish. Then, using the tether as a guide, he swam back to the ship.

Josh heard the airlock close, and Deebee set the craft's speed to 'Forward – slow'. "We bring it with us until we are clear of this turbulence," he explained.

Seezee came back into the cabin and greeted the relief crew. He went to take off his helmet, but Deebee said "Not yet" to him, and "Suit up" to the others. Then he put the ship into hover mode.

The three white-clad aliens moved into the airlock and Josh heard the door whirr open again.

He and Deebee crouched over the screen which now displayed what was happening behind the ship. Seezee and his companions maneuvered the object until it was in full view of the camera. Josh pointed to a golden disk, about twelve inches in diameter, that was fixed below the dish on a sturdy mounting. Its face was covered with etched lines, boxes and a circle.

"Can you get that?" he asked.

None of the aliens was able to remove the disk, and Josh heard Seezee ask what to do.

"Cut it out."

Seezee drew a short instrument that looked like a gun from his suit pocket and pointed it at the object. As he drew a larger circle around the golden disk, a thin gap appeared in the dark metal surrounding it, and the disk began to float free. Seezee grabbed it and passed it to one of the others, before he stowed the laser-gun away. He glanced into the camera and pointed at the rest of the mutilated probe. "It is of no use to us," he said.

"Let it go," Deebee commanded.

Seezee untied the tether and Voyager One drifted away.

When all three aliens were back in the ship, Seezee handed the chunk containing the golden disk to Josh, who examined it carefully. He touched something and a lid sprang open, revealing a grooved round plate.

"It's a record," he said. "How do we play it?"

"You must find out later," Seezee said, while stowing his suit. "But now you must sleep. So must we. It is time for Exgee and Ayjay to take over.

--o--

"Wake up. We land soon."

Josh ran to the flight deck and gazed at the screen. "What are you doing?" he gasped.

The ship was flying at a terrific speed to and fro over Nevada and New Mexico.

"If you wish friends to come, they must see us. We attract their attention."

--o--

Later, in the small hours of a moonlit night, Josh walked to the foot of the ship's ramp, where he breathed in sweet Earth air and fought his disappointment.

Stupid of me. What did I expect – a reception committee? No, of course not.

But he had hoped *someone* would see them land. That *someone* would take him to a police station or a hospital where he could tell his story. He could prove his story by showing them his notebook and camera.

Instead, he stood on the floor of a barren crater, the bag containing his belongings dangling from his wrist. He knew where he was. He'd come to Lunar Crater on a sixth grade field trip. It had to be the loneliest spot in the whole of the United States right then.

Deebee walked down the ramp to stand beside him. "Four of your friends reach us soon," he said. "You must choose. We have room for two. No more."

"Someone's coming?" Josh asked. "Where?"

Deebee pointed south, across the volcanic field. Far away, twin points of light approached through the sage brush.

Josh walked back up the ramp to get a better view; he could just make out an open vehicle bouncing across the rocky, moonlit basin. As it came nearer, he saw four people in the Jeep. The

148

elbows of three of them stuck out like chicken wings while they stared through binoculars. Thin black gun barrels protruded behind their shoulders.

Rifles They must have seen the ship shooting across the sky and have come to investigate. Josh turned to look at the ship glowing behind him. *It won't be hard to find.*

He called Deebee back up the ramp, suddenly feeling uneasy.

Kerpiiiing. Something hit a rock a hundred yards away.

Josh made his bag into a ball and secured it with the drawstring before he tossed it down the ramp.

After rolling and bouncing for several yards, it came to rest in a bare patch of earth.

He reached for Deebee's hand.

"Come on," he said. "Let's go home."

****

FUMBLED FRATRICIDE

Chapter One

Phil was dozing in his rocker on the porch, enjoying the late September sunshine, when he heard music in the distance. He rose stiffly, pinched out his smoke and dropped the stub through a gap between the boards. It landed on a pile of other stubs that sat on the dank earth like a miniature Alpine peak.

His leg ached. He'd broken it when he was a kid and it hadn't been set right. The result was that one leg was shorter than the other and gave him a permanent limp. It ached like hell whenever the weather was on the turn. *It'll rain tomorrow*, he thought.

He limped to the porch rail, leaned on it, and saw a dozen brightly colored balloons coming towards the house. They bobbed and bounced, tethered to the roof of a vehicle that was hidden behind a tall hedge. The music grew louder, the balloons passed the hedge, and he was able to see the minivan that brought the colorful bunch slowly nearer.

As the vehicle progressed down the street, people walked beside it, laughing and shouting. They obscured Phil's line of sight and he couldn't read what was printed on the side of the vehicle until it stopped directly in front of his mother's small graveled front yard. Then he saw the "ASOT" logo - bold, black initials written inside the frame of a television screen. Phil knew the letters stood for "As Seen on Television". His mother had spent far more money than she should have done with this new competitor to Publishers Clearing House, and her kitchen was cluttered with gadgets she would never use.

He limped to the open front door and shouted "Mom!" through the screen. The effort made him cough. He staggered away from the screen and clutched the porch rail until the spasm passed.

Three people came towards him, all smiling. A smarmy-looking man and a short-skirted woman carried a huge, white check between them. A tall man with a camera on his shoulder followed a few paces behind and, at the curb, onlookers clustered round the minivan jostling to get a good view.

Phil turned to call his mother again but found her already beside him, fists level with her chin, looking like a dog begging for a treat. Her petite, scrawny body trembled with excitement.

"I've won! I must've won!" she squealed.

The group of three stopped at the foot of the porch steps.

"Betsy Henderson?" the woman asked.

"Yes. That's me!" Phil's mother did a little dance. "What have I won? Is it the biggie?"

"It certainly is." The smarmy man tugged the huge check away from the woman, and showed it to Betsy. "I'm Jermyn Tredigan, Chairman of ASOT, and I'm honored to present you with our first major prize since we started running our lottery. You've won six thousand dollars a week for the rest of your life and, after you die, your beneficiary will receive the same amount until he or she dies. What do you say to that?"

"Oh, it's wonderful! Just wonderful! I can't believe this is happening to me of all people! And it's great that my boy," – she threw her arms around Phil – "will be provided for after I'm gone."

Phil returned the hug, and then doubled up in a coughing fit.

The man watched him with an amused smile. "Don't take this the wrong way," he said, "but it looks like he's got one foot in the grave already."

"He's stronger than he looks. But what would happen if he did pass before me?"

"You could pick someone else. But only once, mind."

"Well, I've got three more kids to choose from. Hey, when do I get the money?"

"Right now. Come down here and let Troy take our photo. Then Vivian will drive you to the office so you can fill in the forms and we can set up a bank account."

****

Chapter Two

Phil took a long pull of his beer and eyed his siblings. Across the round table, his brother Alan leaned back in his chair, a half-eaten steak on his plate. It had started off the size of a size ten shoe. He sniffed a brandy glass. Other empty wine glasses filled the space near him. He'd taken advantage of the celebration to check out the snobby restaurant's cellar.

Lucinda sat on Phil's left, between him and Alan. She'd been baptized Cynthia but believed that didn't sound right for an actress of her standing. Her family called her either Cindy or just plain Cin. She munched through her salad like a methodical caterpillar and turned her plate at intervals to tackle the mange-tout and curly kale.

Noreen sat on Alan's left, a peeved look on her face. She'd ordered the most expensive fish dish on the menu, rainbow trout, but she'd spotted a bone glisten in the flesh. After she'd eaten the roasted asparagus and the pebble-sized potatoes, she pushed her plate away. The eye of the trout gleamed, as if with suppressed laughter.

To complete the circle, Betsy sat between Noreen on her right and Phil on her left. She wiped her mouth. "I'm done," she said. Her plate was empty apart from a token mouthful of chicken pot pie and a pool of clear gravy. "If I eat that last bit, I'll bust, I declare. No pudding for me but don't let that stop you. This is my treat. Order anything you want."

She picked up her glass and wrinkled her nose in delight as tiny bubbles popped under her nostrils. "But I will finish this. Imagine me, drinking champagne. Never thought I'd see the day." She gulped from the glass and giggled.

Phil frowned. Betsy had had enough. That was clearly indicated by her over-bright eyes and the dark, mottled color staining her hollow cheeks. When her lips missed the rim of the glass and champagne dribbled onto the front of her frilled, satin gown, he gently took the glass from her.

"No more, Mom."

"Aw, don't be mean. Give it back."

She reached for the glass, missed, and her face landed on her plate. Gravy splashed into her stiff, blue-tinted hair-do.

Alan burst out laughing, and Cindy hid her smile behind her napkin. Noreen was not amused. She tutted and said, "Can't take you anywhere, Mother."

Phil pulled Betsy upright again and wiped the mess off her face with his napkin. "Come on. I'm taking you home," he said.

"But I haven't finished eating," Cindy objected, a strip of lettuce hanging from her mouth.

"Carry on, then. You heard Mom. Have what you want. She says to put it on this card." Phil picked up a credit card that had been lying next to his plate and showed it to his siblings. "Who's co-signer on this one?"

"Discover? Not me," Alan said. "I'm on Chase."

"I am," sighed Noreen. "Give it here."

Alan put down his glass. "How will you and Mom get home? I hadn't planned on leaving yet but I suppose I could take you and then come back."

Phil viewed the collection of glasses in front of Alan. "No probs, bro. We'll take a cab."

He helped his mother to her feet, swiveled her towards the exit, and guided her through the tables. He kept her upright and she in turn gave him something to lean on while they weaved their way to the street door.

"Talk about the blind leading the blind," Alan said. He swirled the remaining mouthful of brandy before downing it.

"She's ruined that dress," Noreen said.

Cindy sniffed. "It's hideous, anyway. She should have let me go with her to buy it. Not Phil."

"Do you think she put that on tick, too?" Noreen asked, while playing with the credit card.

"Of course she did," Cindy replied. "So would anyone who's just hit the jackpot. Give her a couple of weeks and she'll start paying off her debts, like she's always promising to do."

Alan snorted. "I'll believe it when I see it. She's never been able to handle money."

A waiter stopped by their table. "Is everything to your satisfaction?" he asked, looking at the half-eaten steak and the untouched trout.

"There's a bone in this." Noreen pushed her plate farther away.

"It's not supposed to be filleted, ma'am."

"Why not? That's dangerous, serving fish with bones in it."

"B-but it's trout. You expect bones---"

"I don't."

"I'm sorry, ma'am. Would you care to order something else?"

"No, I'm done."

"We all are," Alan said, ignoring the fact that Cindy was still eating. He nodded towards Noreen. "She's paying."

Noreen handed the card to the waiter who took it. Swinging his hips, he disappeared behind a tall plant where the register was hidden. A few minutes later, he came back.

"This has been declined," he said, coldly, and placed the disgraced card on the table.

Alan's head jerked up. "Why?"

"Insufficient credit available."

"Oh, my gawd." Alan rubbed his chin. "Her Chase is maxed out, too. What about your card, Cindy?"

Cindy rummaged in her bag. "This is so embarrassing," she muttered. "Here. This is my own card. There's plenty on that." She handed the card to the waiter who disappeared again.

"What do you think it will come to," she asked and twisted her napkin between her fingers.

"Two hundred, easy," was Alan's guess.

"As long as it's less than three fifty. God knows what Trev will say if it's more than that."

"You should've used Mom's," Noreen said.

"No can do. It's maxed out, too. We had back taxes to pay and..." Her voice trailed off when she saw the waiter approaching their table. He gave her the black wallet. She took it, glanced at the total, winced, and signed the slip.

He'd just left when another waiter approached, holding a piece of paper in his right hand.

"Excuse me," he said. "Is this the Henderson table?"

Alan looked up at him. "Yes. Why?"

"I'm afraid there's been an accident, sir."

The waiter passed the note to Alan who glanced at it. Cindy and Noreen leaned towards him, trying to see its contents. He laid the strip of paper on the table and pinned it down with his pudgy fingers while he read the message aloud.

"A car skidded after running a red light and totaled their cab. Both drivers are dead. Mom's in a bad way. They've taken her and Phil to Matthews Medico."

Both women stared at him in disbelief.

"That's **awful**," Cindy said.

"How's Phil?" Noreen asked.

Alan splayed his hands, palms up, while he read the note again.

"It doesn't say."

The waiter moved towards him. "I took the call, sir. The paramedic said your brother is very badly hurt, but he was able to ask for a message to be sent here while you are all together."

He paused, expecting questions. Receiving none, he added, "Will there be anything else?"

The three diners stared at him. They seemed bereft of speech.

Then Alan shook his head and the waiter moved away.

Alan watched him leave. He rubbed his chin, lifted the note, read it again, and then tapped the edge of it on the table in front of him.

"It's bad news," he said, "both of them being hurt. Mom's had a good run. Way more'n her three score years and ten. We just gotta hope Phil dies before her. That way one of us will have a chance at the dough. But if they both die, we won't get a cent."

"Alan!"

"Just facing facts, Cin. Phil's been ill, on and off, since the day he was born. And here he is, knocking on the pearly gates again. If he's gonna meet his Maker, it ought to be before Mom. I vote we make sure he does."

He turned to his left. "What do you think, Nore?"

"You're right. Look how many times we've made plans to bury Phil. If he pulls through after this, his life won't be worth living. We'd be doing him a favor if we, er, helped him on his way."

"I suppose you're right," Cindy muttered, "but it seems mean. And we shouldn't even think about it if Phil's got a good chance of recovery. Anyway, it all depends on how badly Mom's hurt, doesn't it?"

Alan stood and tucked in his shirt tail. "Glad you both see it my way," he said. "Come on. We'd better go to Matthews and find out what state Mom's in before we make any plans."

"I'll drive you there," Noreen said, leaning down to pick up her bag. "No point in taking two cars. Besides, you've had way too much to drink, Al, to get behind a wheel."

"Nah. I'm okay to drive."

"No, you're not. I'll bring you both back here after we've seen Mom. Cindy can drive you home in your car, then take a cab like she did to come here, or ask Trev to pick her up."

"Quite the little mother, aren't we?" Alan sneered.

Noreen shrugged. "Go ahead and drive if you want to. Cin or me will reap the benefit if you die before Mom and Phil."

****

Chapter Three

They sat in a row on a hard, plastic bench in Emergency, waiting for someone to tell them how Mom and Phil were faring. It was bedlam in there due to a multiple pile-up on the Interstate. The staff whisked to and fro as ambulance after ambulance discharged casualties, many in urgent need of attention.

After half an hour of no news, Cindy decided to speed things up. With a lace handkerchief in her hand and her neck sunk into the collar of her faux-fur coat, she went to a nurse who was taking details from a woman in a wheelchair, and tugged her arm.

"I must know what's happened to my dear mother," she sobbed. "I've come all this way. Dropped everything as soon as I heard. Surely somebody can spare a minute, a few seconds---"

Her spiel was cut off by the angry nurse. "Can't you see I'm busy?" she snapped. "Go check at the desk, like everyone else."

Cindy drew herself up to her full height. "How DARE you speak to me like that," she said, haughtily. "I'm Lucinda Meadows---"

"Never heard of you."

Cindy's eyes bulged, but then Alan called "Cin! Cin! Over here."

She looked to where a nurse wearing a dark blue uniform and a white cap stood beside Noreen, Next to her, a tall, dark-haired man had a hand on Alan's shoulder. She'd seen the man before, but where? She tried to place him as she went back to the bench.

"Ah, Lucinda," the man gushed when she reached Alan's side. "I am so sorry to hear of this tragic accident. Your dear mother AND your brother, Philip. I can't believe it. I came as soon as I heard."

"Is she dead?" Cindy blurted. "What about Phil?"

The nurse laid a gentle hand on Cindy's shoulder. "Dinna fret," she said, in a soft Scottish accent. "They're holding their own but ye canna see them the noo. Tomorrow, maybe, but no toneet. We'll keep Mr. Tredigan informed and he can---"

"Who?" Cindy interrupted. "Who's Mr. Tredigan?"

The tall man gave a little cough. "That's me," he said.

"What's so special about you? How did you get to hear about Mom and Phil? Do I know you from somewhere?"

"I'm Jermyn Tredigan. From ASOT. We met two weeks ago in my office."

"ASOT? ASOT?" Cindy mumbled. Then her eyes cleared. "Oh, the lottery." She frowned. "But I still want to know how you get to know what's happened before we do."

He smiled. "Your mother was, er, is our first major prize winner and we've been keeping an eye on her."

"You mean you've been following her?"

"And your brother. Just to make sure they are all right."

"What are you insinuating?" Alan snarled. "Are you suggesting we'd try to hide it if they weren't?"

Jermyn coughed again. "Look at it our way, Mr. Henderson. After your mother's demise, if your brother has predeceased her, one of you will receive her winnings, so it is only logical for us to keep abreast of her state of health. We would not wish any of you to be responsible for reporting a death in the family at such a painful time."

"Why wouldn't we tell you?"

Noreen pursed her lips. "You're so naive, Cin. He's making sure we don't try to hide it if whoever is nominated beneficiary dies after Mom passes, so the money keeps coming. That's the top and bottom of it, isn't it, Mr. Tredigan?"

Jermyn's eyes glittered. "Well, I wouldn't have phrased it quite so bluntly, ma'am, but basically you're right." He paused before he added, "Don't worry. My investigators are trained to be very discreet. You won't even know they are around."

****

Chapter Four

Four weeks later, Noreen went to Matthews Medico to take Phil home. Cindy and Alan were there already, having come to check on Betsy. They met up outside Betsy's side ward.

"She's sleeping or knocked out," Alan said "There's no point going in, Nore. She looks awful but apparently her heart's a lot stronger than we thought."

"Wish mine was." Cindy put a trembling hand on her bosom. "Phil's not the only one with a dodgy ticker."

Alan grinned. "More for one of us if you snuff it before Mom."

"Pig!"

"Just facing facts."

He turned to Noreen. "How long are you looking after Phil?"

"Two weeks. I told my boss I had a family emergency and I'm on compassionate leave. My youngest has promised to look in on hubbie now and again but Joe's not helpless. He's fended for himself before. If I don't get a chance to dispose of Phil while I'm there, one of you will have to do it, but I'll give it my best shot."

Cindy bit her lip. "Sounds like you two are really determined to go through with this. I don't know why you can't let Phil be, especially seeing Mom's not at death's door."

"She might be holding her own right now," Alan retorted, "but it won't last. She's too frail. And Phil might be well enough to go home, but he's even more disabled. We have to take him out of the picture."

"Al's right," Noreen said, "and we ought to do it before he recovers."

"It won't be easy," Cindy argued. "And it's going to have to look natural."

"Of course it will! What do you think I am? An idiot?"

"Now, now, girls." Alan put a hand on each sister's shoulder. "Best of luck, Nore. I'll drop in to see how you're doing. Got to go now. Catch you later."

He walked off down the corridor, waving one arm in the air, fluttering fingers in farewell.

"How much longer is Phil going to be?" Cindy looked at her watch. "I suppose I ought to wait to say goodbye, seeing he knows I'm here. He'll think something's up if I don't."

"Ten minutes ago they were looking for a wheelchair," Noreen said. "Ah! Speak of the devil. Here he comes."

A nurse came along the corridor. Cindy recognized her as the same one who had talked to them in Emergency when Mom and Phil had been admitted. She was pushing a wheelchair in which Phil lolled to one side, his right arm secured against his chest, an overcoat over his pajamas. One foot slid off the rest. Its slipper dropped onto the glossy tiled floor and caught under the wheel. The chair stopped suddenly, the nurse lurched forward, and her chin hit Phil on the back of his head.

Cindy tutted. "It could only happen to you, Phil," she said. She pushed the wheelchair backwards into the nurse's abdomen and retrieved the slipper which she put back on Phil's foot. She stood up, patted her brother's shoulder, and kissed him quickly on the cheek. "Now you take care," she said, wagging a finger. "Don't do anything I wouldn't do."

Phil gave her a goofy grin. "I'll try not to."

He looked up at the nurse. "Sorry, Elsie. I hope that didn't hurt you." He jerked a thumb at the door of the side ward. "Okay if I say goodbye to Mom?"

"Waste of time," Cindy said. "She's fast asleep. She hadn't a clue we were here. See you both later." She picked up her purse and hurried off down the corridor.

Phil pouted. "I still want to see her. Who knows if I'll ever…" His voice trailed off.

The nurse looked at Noreen and raised her eyebrows.

"Oh, all right, but don't be long. I haven't got all day."

Noreen plumped down on a nearby chair and pushed her hair behind her ears in irritation.

Elsie backed the wheelchair into the side ward, bumping the door open with her bottom. She pushed Phil towards the bed, where Betsy laid motionless, eyes closed, her arms resting over the covers.

****

Phil leaned to touch the back of his mother's hand and his chin quivered. "Aw, Mom," he whispered. "It's not fair. Just when things were finally going right for you."

The nurse put an arm along his shoulders. "Would ye like a wee whiley alone?" she asked.

Phil gulped. "Yes, please."

She smiled at him and his heart fluttered. He told himself not to be a fool. There was no way she'd even think of going out with him.

While the door was closing behind the nurse, he heard Noreen ask what was up. He turned back towards the bed to see his mother's eyes were open and she was smiling.

"Mom!" he said, happily. "You've come to."

"Sshhh!" Betsy put an arthritic finger over her lips.

"Why?"

She shushed him again. "They're up to no good, hon."

"Who are?"

Betsy's cold fingers tightened around Phil's, and she tugged him towards her. He fell out of the chair and landed on the bed, his head on her chest.

"Watch your back, hon," she said quietly. "Your sibs can't wait for me to die, but they want you to go first." She cocked her head, listening, and let go of his fingers. Phil heard a rustle behind him and felt strong hands slip under his armpits.

"Och, laddie," Elsie said, as she hauled him back into the chair. "Dinna fret so. Yer Ma will no be leaving us just yet."

Phil put his weight on his good hand, shifted himself into a comfortable position, and watched the nurse brush hair off her patient's forehead.

Betsy's lips curved into a smile. "Thank you, Elsie," she whispered.

Phil's face broke into a huge grin.

Elsie's eyes twinkled as she wagged a finger at him. "Och, mon, is it ye who's won the lottery? Shame on ye, grinning like tha', wi' yer puir wee Ma at death's door."

Phil tried to stifle his smile, but he still looked like the cat left alone with the cream.

"That'll no do. Rub yer eyes, like ye've been greeting."

Phil pushed both fists into his eyes and rubbed hard.

"Aye, that's better," Elsie said, cocking her head to one side. "Dinna let on ter yer kin folk, now, will ye?"

"I won't."

Betsy smiled. "You're a real honey, Elsie"

"Hush, hinnie. Gae back ter sleep." The nurse took the handles of the wheelchair and pushed it out of the side ward.

"What took you so long?" Noreen snapped.

Phil stared at her reproachfully and put his fist to his eye, drawing attention to its redness.

"Sorry, Phil," she muttered. "We've resigned ourselves to losing her. You ought to, too. Face facts. That's what Alan always says. She's too old to get over this."

"I suppose you're right." Phil lowered his head and played with his fingers.

"'Tis time ye were hame," Elsie said, an edge in her voice. "Where are ye parked, Mrs...?"

"Dawtry. I'm in visitors' parking, next to Emergency."

"This way, then."

Elsie pushed the wheelchair along the corridor, while Noreen trailed behind.

"You take care, now, laddie," Elsie said in Phil's ear when they reached Emergency.

Phil frowned, thinking about Mom's warning. "She didn't mean it," he said. "They wouldn't hurt me. Not deliberately."

****

Chapter Five

It was nice to be home, to sleep in his own bed and sit in his rocker on the porch. After not smoking in the hospital, Phil decided not to start again. It took a while to cope with one arm being in a cast, but on the whole he did okay. Several times he told Noreen to go home.

"What kind of a sister do you think I am," she retorted, "leaving you on your own with Mom not here to look after you?"

"She doesn't look after me. I look after her."

"Oh, yeah? Who cleans house, washes dishes, cooks meals?"

"I do. And I don't need you fussing around. You don't have to take any more time off work on my account."

"I said I'd stay two weeks and I will. I'll go home Saturday. What do you want for dinner tonight? We ought to use up the Chinese."

"I don't fancy that again. It's all dried up and we should throw it out. I'll make a stew instead. There's a bit of stewing beef in the freezer."

A gleam crept into Noreen's eyes. "Hmm. Stew. Fine, but you don't want frozen beef. It'll taste like cardboard. I tell you what. I'll ride over to our butcher's first thing in the morning and get Ernie to cut me a nice, fresh strip. And I'll buy some more veg while I'm at it.

We'll have the Chinese tonight. Don't want it to go to waste, do we?"

"Whatever."

Phil headed for the front porch, but after he latched the front door open, he returned to the kitchen.

"About tonight---"

His voice trailed off while he watched his sister.

She was on tiptoes, leaning on the front of the sink, staring out of the window towards the boggy ground at the far end of their unfenced yard. They didn't need a fence down there. Their rental, like all the properties on this side of the street, was bounded by a thickly wooded strip. Beyond the trees lay the river.

Why's she looking down there? Not after blackberries, surely? There can't be many left, and what there are will be rotten.

Phil had made many a pie using the berries that flourished every fall on the brambles that choked the ground between the trees. Mushrooms grew there, too, almost year round, but they weren't edible.

Poisonous mushrooms. Is what she's after? A guy down the street nearly died last year when his wife fried some. Did Mom really mean for me to watch my back?

Noreen dropped onto her heels. She nodded and, as she turned away from the sink, Phil saw a sly look on her face. Quietly, he retraced his steps through the front room and pushed open the screen door. While he limped to his rocker, he tried to quell his anxiety.

I'm being paranoid. She'd never try to kill me, not her own brother.

Or would she?

****

Chapter Six

Phil's bedroom was in the attic, and he reached it via a steep, narrow staircase from the second floor landing. It was a large, gloomy room, bounded by sloping eaves on two sides which reduced the wall space. Its small dormer window looked down onto the porch roof at the front of the house.

When Alan had shared the room with Phil, the window had been Alan's escape route whenever he was grounded. He had screwed a heavy-weight hook into the outside window sill and used a rope with a loop in one end to abseil down to the porch roof. The rope had long since been used for other purposes, but the hook remained.

The sash cords – every one of them – broke after Alan left, and Phil's requests to the landlord to fix the window fell on deaf ears. He had lodged a thick piece of dowel under the top pane which prevented it from sliding down, and the window stayed shut permanently.

On the floor below, Betsy's large bedroom lay below Phil's. To the left was the bathroom (first door left at the top of the stairs). Directly opposite the bathroom, at the other end of the narrow landing, was a small room over the stairs that was only used when guests visited.

Early the next morning, Phil climbed into the bath and tried to look through the narrow sliding window situated a few inches below the ceiling. From there he could look down on the back yard. He wanted to see if Noreen would go to pick mushrooms. However, he was too short, so he put Betsy's squat cork-covered stool-cum-box into the bath and stood on that.

He heard the back door click. Saw Noreen walk down the yard through the long, dew-drenched grass. She splashed through the boggy turf to the trees, ducked her head, and put up a hand to push away low-hanging branches. In her other hand she held a plastic carrier bag.

166

There she goes. Wonder what she'd do if I went down there and asked her what she was doing. Looks like Mom did mean what she said about watching my back.

He went up to his room and finished dressing, all the while wondering how to avoid eating the mushrooms if Noreen did put some in the stew. Then he went back to the landing and waited for Noreen to return. He heard the back door open. After giving her time to kick off her gumboots, he went downstairs. When he pushed open the kitchen door she was shoving the plastic bag into the vegetable drawer of the fridge.

A strand of sticky spider web glistened on the back of her short hair-do. When Phil moved near her to brush it off, he saw the yellowy-brown body of a fat spider. Its spindly legs high-stepped over a hair, then headed for his sister's neck.

Phil grinned and stayed his hand. Noreen had a thing about spiders. She had feared and hated them ever since she was a kid.

"Morning, Nore," he said, and poured himself a cup of coffee.

"Morning, Phil."

She twitched her shoulder, and brushed her hand against the back of her neck. The spider ran over her hand and down her sleeve.

"Aaagh! Get it off! Get it off!" She danced around the kitchen, shaking her left arm.

"Stand still, woman. Let me get at it."

Phil took his time while he coaxed the spider onto the back of his free hand.

"Wow, he's a whopper. Look, Nore."

"Get it out of here."

"I dunno. I think we ought to keep it."

Her eyes opened in horror.

"We wouldn't have flies, not with a brute like this around."

167

Tears ran down Noreen's face. "You're a rotten pig. You know I can't stand them."

"Calm down." Phil opened the back door. He flicked the spider into space, and closed the door again.

"That was a real biggie," he said. "Wonder where it came from. Did you leave Mom's window open last night?"

"No, er, um," Noreen dithered, obviously unwilling to admit she'd been outside. "I suppose I must've done. How else could it have gotten in?"

Phil shrugged and lifted his cup. "Ugh. It's cold." He poured the coffee in the sink.

"It's yesterday's. I'll make you a fresh one. What are you going to do today?"

"Laundry's piling up. I need some clean shirts."

"Have fun."

Noreen knocked the used grounds into the pedal bin, emptied another sachet of coffee into the basket and half-filled the carafe. "Why do you buy this weak stuff?" she grumbled after she hit the "Brew" button.

"I don't like it strong."

"I'll get myself a decent cup while I'm out. Right, I'm off. Do you want anything?"

"No. I'm all set."

Phil waited for the coffee to brew, made himself a cup, then limped out onto the porch and settled himself in his rocker. He pulled his phone out of his pocket and placed it on the small table next to him. After taking a long draught of coffee, he picked up his phone and made his daily call to the hospital. As usual, he had a long wait until Elsie came on the line.

"Yer Ma's had a good neet," she told him. "If she keeps this up, she'll be on her way hame afore ye know it."

"Honestly?"

"I wouldna lie to ye, laddie. To yer kin? Maybe. But I'll no lie to ye."

Phil imagined the pretty woman talking to him on the other end of the line. "Aw, Elsie, you're the best," he breathed.

He heard her happy laugh. "Ye're no so bad yerself," she said, before she clicked off.

∗∗∗∗

Chapter Seven

It was gone ten when Noreen came home. Straight away she set about preparing dinner.

"Where's your crockpot?" she asked while kneeling in front of the cupboard under the sink. Most of the pots and pans that normally lived in there were scattered around her.

"We haven't got one."

"You're kidding me." Noreen half-turned to look up at him. "How can I make stew without a crockpot?"

"You'll have to use Mom's old iron pot. Here, I'll get it. It's bloody heavy."

Noreen shuffled backwards on her bottom, out of his way.

The pot lived on the bottom of the unit, right at the back. Phil knelt and groped underneath the top shelf with his left hand, seeking an ear-shaped handle. He found it and tugged.

The pot didn't budge.

"Blast it. Bloody thing's stuck."

He laid flat on the floor, his right cheek squashed against it while he looked into the cupboard. It was an awkward position to be in, and the cast on his right arm dug into his belly. His head began to throb.

"Does it have to be stew for dinner," he gasped, and turned onto his back. His foot hit a lid and sent it skidding.

"Look out!" Noreen said, irritably.

Phil's heart beat erratically. He lifted his heavy right arm onto his heaving chest and his fingers plucked at his shirt. Panic rose inside him. The last time he'd felt like this he'd ended up in hospital. He took deep breaths and tried to stay calm.

Noreen bent over him. Even through half-closed eyelids, he didn't miss the gleam of delight in his sister's eyes. He realized that, with a little more effort on his part, there wouldn't be any need for her to have picked the mushrooms.

Heck! I'm doing the bloody job for her.

"We'll have something else for dinner," he said and tried to sit up, but Noreen pushed him down again.

"I'm not spending my hard-earned cash on good stew meat, not to mention all those veggies, and not have stew," she said. "God, Phil. You're such a wimp."

The short rest had given Phil's heart time to slow to a near-normal beat, and he breathed more easily. But he wasn't ready to tax that dodgy organ any further, so he took his time. He swiveled round on his backside, still lying on his back, and put his left arm into the cupboard again. When he touched the pot, it moved slightly. He pushed again, and, with a creak, the bottom of the pot lifted an inch, revealing a sticky, rust-colored ring.

He gritted his teeth and pushed yet again. That freed the pot. He curled his fingers behind its fat, black belly and tugged the pot towards him. Inch by inch it moved nearer until it was at the front of the cupboard. Then he sat up and was able to drag the blasted thing onto the kitchen floor.

The effort made him cough. While he sat, hacking and spluttering, he heard Noreen pick up the pans and lids. However, she didn't touch the stew pot.

The spasm passed. Phil looked up and saw the disappointment in Noreen's eyes.

He climbed awkwardly to his feet, and bent again to lift the heavy pot with his left hand. Noreen's foot was inches away. He fought the urge to drop the pot on it and break a few toes.

Better not. Don't want to give her any more ideas. One clout from that and I'm a goner.

He dumped the pot in the sink, and then flopped onto a chair.

Noreen washed the pot out before she cut the stew meat into perfectly square cubes.

Phil sat at the table and watched her. "We'll be eating stew all week," he said. "You've got enough beef there to feed an army."

She looked up. "Didn't I tell you? Alan's coming for dinner after he's looked in on Mom. You know how much he can put away and he's always on the scrounge since he's been on his own. I think he survives on burgers or Chinese."

Interesting. If Alan's coming to dinner, she won't put any mushrooms in the stew. I wonder how she's gonna get round that.

"Do you want a hand?" he asked. "I could do the veggies."

Noreen laughed. "One-handed? I don't think so."

"Just 'cause my arm's in a cast doesn't mean I can't use my hand."

"You really are an independent sod, aren't you? Thanks but no thanks. Go have a smoke."

Phil went out to the porch and leaned back in his rocker. He stared at the spider webs on the underside of the porch and tried to think of a good excuse for skipping dinner.

****

Chapter Eight

"Dinner's up," Noreen called.

Phil could see button mushrooms in the stew along with carrots, celery, potatoes and peas. He wondered where the wild mushrooms were until he noticed that Noreen had fried a pile of onions in a separate skillet. While she was ladling a large helping of them into Phil's bowl, he saw black segments of mushroom between the yellow strands of onion.

"Dig in," she said. "Don't wait for me." She went to the stove to make her own helping, and turned to catch Phil watching her. "What are you staring at?"

"Aren't you having any onions?"

"No. Don't like them. Never have done. Go on. Get stuck in. It'll go cold."

She placed a smaller serving of stew on the table opposite him, dragged a chair away, and prepared to sit down.

Footsteps sounded from the front room. Alan strode into the kitchen. He rubbed his hands and smacked his lips.

"Hey! What's this? You didn't wait for me?"

"There's plenty. If you're hungry, grab mine. I'll make myself another bowl."

She turned back to the stove and Alan sat down. He frowned at the small helping, bent across the table and ogled the huge helping in front of Phil. He winked, took his brother's bowl and replaced it with Noreen's. The exchange was so swift that it was completed before the chunk of meat on Phil's fork reached his mouth.

Phil put down his fork and stared at his brother.

Alan shoveled stew into his mouth. "This is delish, Nore," he mumbled, gravy dribbling down his chin.

Noreen carefully carried her bowl to the table and sat down with Phil on her left, Alan on her right. She lifted her spoon, but paused with it in mid-air and looked at Phil. "Eat up. You didn't have to wait for me."

"Great stew, Nore," Alan said, after he gulped another laden spoonful. "Sorry I cut you off this morning. I heard the bit about coming to dinner but couldn't chat right then. Not a good time. Was that all you wanted?"

Noreen blinked. "You didn't hear me say we were having stew?"

"No. Just the invite to dinner."

Phil had heard warning in his sister's voice. He watched her tap a finger on the side of her bowl as if she were sending Alan an urgent message in Morse code.

"I thought you understood me," she said.

Phil drew a breath between his teeth. Nore had doctored the stew and now Alan was eating what she'd given him. *Serves him right.* He jabbed another chunk of meat and relished chewing it. "Got to admit you make a mean stew, Nore," he said, before he turned to Alan and asked "How's Mom?"

"Ready to come home, apparently. They asked me to line up some home care for her. You know what she needs, Nore, better than me. Can you see to it?"

Noreen was still tapping her bowl.

Phil coughed to stop his brother looking her way. "Why don't we get her a private nurse?"

"And where do we find one of those," Alan demanded.

"It was just a thought. Mom likes Elsie, the nurse at Matthews. I bet – if we offer her enough – she'd be willing to come and live here. We've got a spare room."

"Not a bad idea," Noreen agreed. "Can we afford her?"

Alan pushed his now-empty bowl away. "Mom's loaded. She can't have spent much while she's been laid up. Let's see." He counted on his fingers. "Six, no seven weeks at six grand a week. She should have forty grand at least, even taking that meal and what she bought in the first week into account. I was thinking of asking her for a sub."

"Forget it," Phil said, sharply. "Except for not owing anything on her cards, she's no better off than she was before she won the money."

"How do you know what she's got in the bank?"

"I handle her account. She asked me to do it a year ago."

"Why you? Why not me or Nore or Cin?"

"She trusts me. She knows I won't rob her."

Alan's eyes flashed. "And we would?"

When Phil kept silent, he added, "So what IS she worth?"

"About two grand."

Alan pushed his chair back, leaned on the table and glared at him. "Is that all?" he roared.

Noreen stared at him, too. "Where's it all gone?"

"On her credit cards. Took thirty six grand. And I closed them, so no-one can run them up again. Then there was---"

"Hold it right there." Alan stood, rubbed his chin, and then wagged his forefinger at Phil. "Let me get this straight. You've closed her cards. Now WE can't buy sod-all but YOU get whatever you want, whenever you want!"

"Right. Except it's what Mom wants. Not what I want."

"Liar!"

"Calm down, Alan." Noreen frowned at Alan, and then turned to Phil. "I bet Mom wanted the cards paid off in case she died. As co-signs we'd all have been lumbered, wouldn't we?"

Phil nodded, and put down his fork.

Alan sat down again, his anger fading. "Well, I suppose she meant well. And it'll soon mount up again. Even if she only lasts a couple of months she'll be worth about fifty grand and, if she passes, one of us, er, I mean Phil, will get the six grand a week."

Phil bit his lip. "There'll be her hospital bill."

"No, there won't," Noreen contradicted. "Matthews will waive that. She's on Medicare."

"Makes no difference," Phil retorted. "They'll probably waive mine seeing I'm on Disability. Got no other income. But with six grand a week coming in, there's no way they'll waive Mom's."

Alan stared at him in disbelief. Then his face screwed as if he were suddenly in pain. He doubled up and hugged his belly.

"O-o-o-o-h," he groaned. "O-o-o-o-h."

Noreen reached to touch his upper arm. "What's wrong, Al?"

"God - the pain - O-o-o-o-h."

Noreen's eyes flicked from his empty bowl to Phil's and back again. She shook Alan's arm. "You didn't---. Say you didn't---"

"Didn't what?" Alan lifted an agonized face to look at her.

Noreen's finger jerked back and forth between the bowls.

Understanding dawned in Alan's eyes. He sprang away from the table, knocking his chair over in his haste. Then he staggered out of the kitchen into the front room.

Noreen leapt over the fallen chair and caught up with him. With her hands on his shoulders, she hustled him towards the open front door.

Phil swung round in his chair to listen. He heard Noreen say "Go to Emergency and have your stomach pumped. Hurry! Hurry!"

His heart pounded. *She did it! She really did it! That should be me holding my guts. Maybe Al can take it. He's strong as a horse. And hey, that other guy didn't die. P'raps Al won't, either.*

175

He heard choking coming from the front yard and hurried to see what was going on. From behind the screen door he saw his brother spew into the pea gravel.

Noreen stood to one side of Alan, distancing herself from the brown stream of vomit. When it dwindled, she leaned forward and thumped Alan on the back. "You stupid sod," she hissed. "I told you to take mine, not his."

Alan wiped his mouth with the back of his hand and stumbled to his car. With a screech of tires, he reversed out of the yard so fast that his car's rear end smashed into the side of a vehicle parked on the opposite side of the road.

The owner of the damaged vehicle ran out of his house, but arrived too late to stop Alan's car fishtailing away. He hurled abuse at Noreen and threatened to call the cops.

She didn't respond. She balanced on one foot and used the other to cover the vomit with gravel. Once the smelly pool was hidden, she trudged back to the house and up the porch steps.

Phil held the screen door open for her.

She didn't thank him. Just walked like a zombie through the front room and into the kitchen.

Phil let the screen door clang shut behind him. He unhooked the front door from the eye-bolt that kept it open most of the day and shut that door, too. He limped into the kitchen and found Noreen inspecting the dregs in Alan's bowl. She bit her lip and looked towards Phil who adopted what he hoped was an innocent expression. He didn't fool her. It was obvious from her scared eyes and trembling hands that she knew he knew what she'd done. He turned away, still trying to come to terms with the fact that his sister had actually tried to kill him.

****

Chapter Nine

They cleared the meal away in silence. Noreen washed up while Phil dried. The big iron pot still held enough stew for two more helpings and neither of them touched it. Noreen flushed the rest of the fried onions down the sink, and didn't bother to hide the finely chopped pieces of mushroom. Then she scrubbed and scrubbed the skillet as if it were her hand and she were Lady Macbeth.

When all was tidy, they went into the front room. Phil sat in his usual fireside chair, his back to the window, while Noreen perched on the edge of Mom's. He pretended to doze but now and then stole a glance at his sister. She sat, feet together, clasping and unclasping her hands, staring at the window.

Half an hour passed, then another, and not a word was spoken. Phil squirmed in his chair. He couldn't stand the tension any longer. "Why?" he asked. "Why try to bump me off?"

Noreen looked down at her hands and picked at a thumb nail. "It was Alan's idea. He said if Mom died and straight after, you did, too, no-one would get anything."

"You're despicable. The lot of you."

Noreen tossed her head. "You're just as bad," she retorted.

"Me! How do you work that out?"

"You knew. But you still let Alan take your bowl."

That's right. I did. Jeez, I am as bad as you. "What makes you think I knew?"

"That spider could only have come from the yard. You must've twigged I'd been out there."

"To get the mushrooms."

"Yeah. Omigod, do you think Al's going to be all right?"

"Probably. He spewed it all up and he's strong as a horse."

"I couldn't bear to think I'd killed him."

"But it's okay to kill me?"

"I told you. It was his idea."

An uneasy silence shrouded them again. It was broken ten minutes later when they heard footsteps crunching gravel. The unseen visitor rapped loudly on the siding beside the screen door.

Noreen didn't stir.

Phil stood up. "I'll go."

Outside, a heavy-chested cop eyed him through the screen.

Phil squinted at the officer's badge. "Sergeant Palmer?"

"That's right, sir. Are you Mr. Henderson? Mr. Philip Henderson?"

"Yeah. That's me. Is something wrong?"

"'Fraid so, sir. It concerns Mr. Alan Henderson---."

"My brother?" Phil interrupted. "You'd better come in."

He stepped back while holding the front door open for the officer. After he shut it, he pointed to Noreen. "My sister, Noreen Dawtry."

She stood and tucked her hair behind her ears. "What is it, officer? I heard you mention Alan. Is he all right?"

"No, ma'am. 'Fraid not. Your brother crashed his car into a wall at Matthews Medico. He's in pretty bad shape with both legs broken. They found his auto insurance card in the glove box and the clerk on the desk remembered he was a regular visitor. Been going there to see his mother, she said."

"Mom was in a bad accident a couple of months ago."

"You were involved in that, too, weren't you, sir?"

"Yeah. I was discharged ten days ago."

"Was your brother making his regular visit to your mother tonight then?"

"Not really," Noreen said. She looked at Phil. "We should never have let him go. Not while he was that riled up."

"Riled up? What upset him, ma'am?"

"He wanted some of Mom's money – she won the lottery, you know – but Phil said he'd have to clear it with her first."

She dropped her head in her hands and said, through her fingers, "You should've said yes, Phil. You know what Al's like when he can't get his own way."

Phil stared at her. *You cunning bitch. Putting the blame on me.*

The officer put his thumbs in his belt and addressed Phil. "Why is it up to you, sir?"

"I look after Mom's affairs."

"So he went to Matthews to ask her himself?"

Phil and Noreen exchanged glances then Phil said, "Um, it looks like it."

The cop shook his head. "Obstinate guy, eh? I pity his wife."

"He hasn't got one," Phil said. "Not any more. She divorced him years ago."

"What about family?"

"Just us, Mom and Cindy, our other sister."

The officer rubbed his chin. "There'll be proceedings," he said. "He damaged four vehicles, including an ambulance, before crashing into that wall and people will want to make claims. You seem to be in charge, sir. Should we tell them to contact you?"

Phil shrugged. "I guess. I don't suppose you want to, Nore?"

"No. And Cindy won't either."

"It's up to me, then. What do I have to do?"

"We'll ask the claimants to contact you at this address. Just give them details of your brother's insurance."

"I don't know who he's with."

"You can pick up his card from Matthews. They also want to know about his health insurance."

"We'd best go see him, Nore, soon as poss." Phil scratched his neck and looked at the officer. "Will they let us? Is he conscious?"

"He's very badly hurt. That's all I've got in my report."

****

"Only one of you," the nurse said, when they reached Emergency.

"We've got to have his insurance details," Noreen said, "for the claims. Can I look through his wallet to see if his card's in it?"

The nurse frowned. "Your brother's clothing is in a plastic bag right now. It would be most unpleasant to touch. He appears to have vomited copiously and there's a lot of blood."

"Eeeeew." Noreen shivered.

"Besides," the nurse added, "the police will probably want to inspect it if he doesn't make it. It's a possibility."

"I just want a quick word with him," Phil muttered. "It's because of me he's in here."

"Really?" The nurse stared at him. "Did you have an argument or something?"

"Sort of."

She pursed her lips, and beckoned a colleague.

"Take Mr. Henderson to see his brother. Let him have five minutes, max, and if the patient even looks like getting agitated, make Mr. Henderson leave, immediately."

"Can't I talk to him on my own?"

"After what you just said? No. Definitely not."

Phil stood by the side of the gurney, regarding Alan. He was lying on his back, a bandage swathed around his head, his chin tucked into a huge neck brace. From the waist down, the bed covers hung over a cage, keeping them from touching his legs.

"Hi, bro." Phil's finger tips touched his brother's shoulder.

Alan swung his eyes to look sideways at him. Guilt and fear shone in them.

"Nore made a great stew, didn't she?" Phil said. "But you know what they say. Best laid plans, and all that."

"Not planned," Alan whispered. "It was a-a game."

"A game? Honest? Can anybody play? My turn next, then."

Alan closed his eyes and tried to turn away.

The nurse tapped Phil's back. "You'd better leave," she said.

****

Chapter Ten

Phil limped back to the desk.

"Let's go see Mom and get this over with," he said to Noreen.

When they stepped out of the elevator on Mom's floor, Elsie was passing. She looked at Phil, her eyes asking questions.

He didn't see her. He pushed Noreen onto a chair outside the ward. And did it so roughly, she nearly toppled off the chair.

Elsie looked at him in surprise.

"Hey! Watch it," Noreen protested.

"I'll go in first," Phil said, "then you. She's going to be real upset about Alan. And what do I say happened? That he ate something that disagreed with him? That he crashed into a brick wall and damn near killed himself? That---."

181

"Say he was in an accident," Noreen interrupted. "Nobody's fault. At least, not his."

Phil snorted. "Right!" he sneered, before pushing open the door and limping into the ward.

****

Elsie walked down the corridor but, a few yards farther on, she turned, tiptoed back towards Noreen, then slipped into the empty ward next to Betsy's. She stood just inside the door and, while holding it open a crack, watched Phil's sister rummage in her big, leather bag until she drew out her phone.

Noreen pressed a button. "Cin?" she asked.

"Hi." Cindy spoke loudly, cheerfully. She started to chat until Noreen butted in.

"For crissakes," she hissed into the screen, "shut up, will you? It's all gone wrong."

Elsie heard a gasp from the phone. Then Noreen carried on. "Alan ate Phil's stew---."

Cindy interrupted with, "How did that happen?"

"Phil let him swap bowls when my back was turned. Looks like he'd been warned we were out to get him. Don't know how. Anyway, Al was in agony. He spilled his guts in Mom's front yard then drove here to Matthews to get his stomach pumped. Trouble is, he crashed into a wall when he got here and now he's in Intensive Care. He might not pull through. Phil's telling Mom about it right now. She's going to go berserk. You know how she is about Al. Her favorite. Her baby. Makes me want to puke."

Elsie couldn't make out Cindy's reply.

Noreen nodded and said, "Of course the shock will set Mom right back. It could even kill her so now we've got to get rid of Alan, too, that is, if the crash doesn't do it for us. If he looks like pulling through, I'll see he doesn't."

"How?" came from the phone.

"I'll think of something."

Elsie couldn't make sense of Cindy's mumbled reply.

"What?" Noreen gasped. "Are you crazy? Phil knows what I did. He's got to go before he blabs to the cops. But I've done my bit. **You** see to Phil. I'll see to Alan."

The ward door opened and Phil came out, his head bowed.

Noreen stood up. "Gotta go, Cin. Catch you tomorrow," she said, and dropped her phone into her bag. She turned to her brother. "So, how is she?"

Phil rubbed his neck with his left hand and gulped before he said, "Crying her bloody eyes out. She wants to go see him. I've buzzed for the nurse."

"Hey! You could've waited 'til I'd been in."

"Sorry. Didn't think. Nip in quick, before anyone comes."

Noreen grabbed her bag and sidled into the ward.

Phil rubbed his neck again, and dropped onto the chair that she had vacated. He sat with his hands between his knees and stared at the floor.

Elsie felt her pager vibrate. She glanced at the small screen then strode out of her hiding place. She put a hand on Betsy's door, but turned to Phil, as if she'd just spotted him.

"Phil? What are ye a-doin' here? Was it ye that called me fer yer Ma?"

Phil nodded.

"What's gang awry?"

"I had to give her some bad news. Real bad news 'bout Alan. She wants to go see him. He's in Intensive Care."

"Here? In our ICU?"

Phil nodded again, and blurted, "It should've been me down there. Noreen tried to, to---"

Elsie bit her lip. "Och, laddie. Yer Ma did warn ye."

"I didn't believe her. Well, would you?"

Elsie shook her head. She went to push the door open.

Phil jumped up and reached for her arm.

"Before you go in. I said Al's been in a road accident. Don't tell her different, will you? She warned me, but I don't think either of us believed they'd really try to get rid of me."

"Gae ter the police. Ye canna let them get away wi' attempted murder. I'll back ye up."

"I don't think they'll try again. Not after this."

Elsie hesitated. "Let's hope so," she said, "but it wouldna harm ter keep yer distance from yer kinfolk fer a wee whiley."

****

Noreen came out of the ward a few moments after Elsie had gone in. "That bossy bitch!" she complained. "Sent me away as if I had no right to be in there."

"What's going to happen?" Phil asked, rubbing his neck again.

"She's arranging for an orderly to take Mom down to Intensive Care."

"Do you want to see Al again?"

"Not tonight. I'll come tomorrow."

"Can we go home, then?"

"Sure. I'll run you back." Noreen bit a finger nail. "Look, Phil, I know I said I'd stay 'til Saturday, but there's things I want to do. Will you be all right at home on your own?"

Phil heaved a sigh of relief. "No probs. I told you I don't need looking after. I can manage."

He almost said 'thanks' but decided not to when he remembered why she'd offered to look after him in the first place. Jeez, if he'd eaten her stew, it would have been him in Matthews Medico, not Alan.

****

Chapter Eleven

Cindy sat opposite Noreen in the small cafe. She pulled a couple of sachets of sweeteners out of the tub before she pushed it over to Noreen.

"Really, Nore," she said, stirring her coffee. "I thought you had more imagination than that. The stew would've been the first thing the cops would've checked."

"I didn't put the bad mushrooms in the stew. I cooked them separate."

"Still it's lucky Al crashed the car and nearly did himself in. It diverts suspicion."

"I didn't have many options. Poison was the only thing I could think of. What will you do? It's your turn next."

"I'll concentrate on his weak point."

"Which one? He's got half a dozen."

Cindy sniffed. "Don't be dim, Nore. It's obvious."

"Not to me, it's not."

"His heart. He's got a bad heart, same as me."

"Oh, that's right. Hey, you should've seen him struggling to pull Mom's old pot from under the sink. Big, bloody heavy thing. I thought he was going to do himself in right there and then. Shame he didn't. Alan would still be okay if he had."

"So he's stressed out?"

"Yeah. Big time, and this business with Al can't be doing him any good."

"It's not helping me, either. I had a nasty turn when you told me. Made my heart go boom, booma, boom. Now, how can I arrange to give him a really bad shock?"

The sisters fell silent, thinking.

Noreen downed her coffee, and then snapped her fingers.

"You'll have to go stay with him, like I did."

"No way. He'll suspect something if I offer to look after him straight after you go home."

"Now you're being dim. It's Mom you'd be going there for, not him. She was ready for discharge and they asked Al to find a home help for her. Somebody's got to get her room ready before she leaves Matthews. Phil's arm is still in plaster, so he can't do it. You wouldn't have to take time off work, like I did."

"I've got rehearsals, but I suppose I could fit them in. Let me think about this."

"Well, while you're thinking, I'll go see Alan and get his insurance details. If I'm allowed to see him, that is. I hope he is insured. You know Al. He hates parting with money, but doesn't mind spending other people's."

"True. Give me a call before you leave there and let me know how they're both doing."

"Will do. So long."

****

When Noreen went into Matthews Medico's ICU, the woman at the desk told her Alan had been moved into a ward and that he was as comfortable as could be expected. "But," she added, "it's a safe bet he'll be a guest of this establishment until well after Christmas."

"How's my Mom, Betsy Henderson?" Noreen asked. "They said she was ready to come home but she was real upset when Alan crashed his car last night. Is she still fit to be discharged?"

"Just a minute. I'll speak to the ward."

From where Noreen stood at the desk, she could see a long corridor that led to X-Ray and other offices, and she watched people moving back and forth along it. A tall man came out of an elevator and turned towards the exit, allowing her only a brief glance at his face, but she knew him. Of course! Jermyn whatever his name was. Come to check on Alan, no doubt. She sniffed, and then realized the desk clerk was speaking to her.

"Your Mom's fit to go. Who's coming to pick her up?"

"My sister, Lucinda Meadows. She's an actress."

"I know Cynthia. Went to school with her. A pain in the neck and a proper drama queen." The clerk bent towards Noreen and said, quietly, "Do you know what the cast call her?"

"No. Do tell."

"Loose in da madhouse."

"Loose in da---. Oh my," Noreen covered her mouth with her hand and giggled. "That's a good one. I'll have to tell Alan."

"I know Alan, too. From school. He was a couple of grades below me. Tell him Theo Chambers said Hi."

"Will do. Which ward is he in? Can I go see him now?"

"Sure. He's in Don Travers, on three. The elevator's down there." Theo leaned over the desk and pointed to the sign.

Alone in the elevator, Noreen thought about the man she'd seen leaving it. She was sure it was Jermyn. Who had he come to see? Alan or Mom? Heck, I hope they're both all right.

****

Alan was in a cubicle at the end of the ward and it took Noreen a few minutes to realize that the guy with the big neck brace and strips of Band-Aid across his chin was her brother.

"Hi," she said, plumping down in the chair beside him. "They took the bandage off your head. Must mean you're not so badly hurt after all. How are you feeling?"

Alan grunted. "Rough. Broke both legs, but my skull's not fractured, like they thought. Can't get out of bed. I have to call a bloody nurse when I want to go."

"You're lucky you're alive. Hey, I'm sorry about the stew, Al, but I honestly thought you'd got the message. Couldn't believe it when I realized you'd swapped bowls. Did anyone ask what made you throw up?"

"'Course they did. I said I'd had some rotten fish. They seemed to buy it."

"Good. I need your health insurance details. Where do I find them?"

"There's a card in my wallet."

"And that is---?"

"With my clothes. In the nightstand."

Noreen swiveled round, opened the door of the small cabinet and pulled out a bulging white plastic bag tagged with Alan's name. She loosened the draw string and immediately pulled back, wrinkling her face in disgust.

"Phew! It's rank!"

"Can you get them cleaned up? That's my good suit in there."

"Must I? Don't you keep a copy of your health cards somewhere else?"

"In a file at home. Oh, Jeez, Jinja! I forgot about Jinja!"

"Jinja?"

"My pooch. He'll be starving. Crossing his legs. Can you go get him and look after him?"

"No, Al. I've got enough on my plate without adding a mangy dog to the mix."

"He's not mangy. Big and ugly, I grant you, but not mangy. Please, Nore? Until you find somewhere that'll have him? He gets stroppy when he's with other dogs and he's banned from the kennels nearest me, but you can handle him. Please, Nore? I don't want to have him put down. Mom and Phil can't have him, and Cindy won't. And he's all I've got for company."

"My heart bleeds for you."

"Please?"

"Oh, I suppose so. Against my better judgment. Gimme a key."

Alan grinned. "It's in my pocket. With my wallet."

A bell sounded and Noreen looked over her shoulder to see other visitors bending over patients, patting shoulders or kissing goodbyes.

"I'm a pushover," she grumbled as she laced her fingers in the drawstring of the smelly bag.

"No, you're not. You're the best," Alan said. "But you owe me one for putting me in here."

"That was your own fault. By the way, have you had any other visitors today?"

"No. Why?"

"I thought I saw that guy from ASOT. You know. The lottery."

"He was probably checking on Mom. She's due to go home. Are you taking care of that?"

"No, Cindy is. She'll stay with Mom 'til she figures out what to do about Phil."

"Here's hoping she does a better job of it than you."

"Beast!"

"Just joking. Like I said, you're the best. Don't forget about Jinja."

"I won't. I'll come see you tomorrow if I can."

Noreen trotted out of the ward, past grinning patients, holding the plastic bag at arms' length in front of her and fanning her nose with her free hand.

****

Chapter Twelve

While Noreen visited Alan, Cindy went to the public library, intending to read up on what induces heart attacks but didn't find much in the way of instruction manuals. She tackled her search unwillingly. She didn't want to execute Phil but, having promised Noreen and Alan that she would, she felt she had to give it a go.

The books she chose revealed that most heart attacks were caused by blood clots, disease or stress. Nothing promised to induce death in any other way that appeared completely natural. She was disappointed. She wanted to do the job right first time. If she failed, she mustn't leave evidence pointing back to her. Not like Noreen and her stupid stew.

She was leaving the library when an idea presented itself to her. She stopped walking and bit the nail of her forefinger.

I know. I'll scare him. Phil's terrified of the paranormal. I'll get him to watch one of my DVDs. Then, a couple of hours after he goes to bed, I'll spook him. Make out I'm a demon or an evil spirit. I could use Trev's Halloween mask. That should do it. It scared the shit out of the local kids. If that fails, Al or Nore will have to try again. It was their idea anyway. Poor Phil. What's he done to anyone?

Over the years Cindy had collected DVDs in which characters had succumbed to heart attacks. She'd bought them hoping they'd help her recognize signs of an imminent attack. Apparently, however, she could be taking her last breath right now and not know it. One minute, making out. The next, ashes to ashes and all that. The only thing she had learned was that people can die of heart failure if they are frightened badly enough.

****

"What's to stop me going home now?" Betsy asked the next day after Elsie and Cindy came into the ward, and Elsie confirmed she would be discharged at the weekend.

Cindy sat on the side of her bed. "It'll give me three days to give your room a good clean. Nore didn't touch it, you know, when she was there, even though she slept in it."

"It doesn't have to be that clean," Betsy argued. "Phil's done a good enough job for the past ten years."

Cindy interrupted. "But his arm's still in plaster and men can't clean like women. Anyway, it's about time it had a good going-over. And I'll clean the spare room, too. That's not been used for years. I bet the dust is an inch thick in there. It'll bring on my asthma."

"Huh! You're too picky. I'm fed up with being in hospital and I want to go home. Mind you, I'll miss you, Elsie, honey. I'll miss you big time."

The nurse smiled. "'Tis a sweetheart ye are, hinny. I'll miss ye, too."

She turned to Cindy. "The almoner asked yer brother, Alan, to see about home help fer yer Ma before she leaves here. Did he do oot about it?"

"Not that I'm aware of," Cindy said. "That's another reason for you to stay put a couple more days, Mom. It'll give me time to check it out."

****

Phil was enjoying a beer in the front room, his feet on the coffee table, when he heard Cindy's car pull up in the front yard.

She struggled up the steps, her arms wrapped around two enormous pillows. They slid out of her grasp and landed on the porch. "Open up, Phil," she shouted as she banged on the door, before she ran down the steps to get more items out of her car.

Phil sighed, put down his beer, and limped towards the front door. He dropped the hook into the eye bolt, and stood shivering on the porch while he held the screen door open for her.

"What the heck's all this?"

Cindy dropped a big cardboard box inside the doorway and gave it a kick. It skidded into the room. She picked up the pillows. "Mom's due home Saturday and I've come to make her room nice. Sorry to barge in on you without warning but it was only settled this morning. I'll sleep in the spare room. I've brought my own bedding."

Phil shut the doors and turned to face her, rubbing his arms to warm them. "How long are you staying? Not that it makes any difference to me."

"Until we get a home help organized for Mom."

"We don't need one. I can manage."

"Don't be stupid. Your arm's in plaster. And what happens if you get sick or need help?"

Phil immediately went on red alert. *So I'm going to get sick, am I?* "I'll do the cooking."

Cindy shrugged. "Fine by me. Trev does it at home."

"And he's okay with you being here?"

"Well, he's not ecstatic but who else is there? Nore's done her bit and Al's out of action for Lord knows how long."

"Who's looking after Jinja?"

"Nore."

"Sooner her than me. He's a liability, that dog."

"He should be in kennels but not many round here will take him. He's got a bad rep. Nore's looking for somewhere."

Phil went back to his chair and lifted his can. "I'll give you a hand taking stuff upstairs when I've finished this."

"Oh, is that a beer? Got one for me?"

"Sure. There's a six pack at the bottom of the fridge."

After Cindy fetched her beer, she relaxed in Betsy's rocking chair and sucked the cold drink straight out of the can.

"We do have glasses if you want one," Phil said. "You don't have to slum."

"Nah. Tastes better out of the can and saves washing up."

Phil raised his eyebrows. That didn't sound like his finicky sister. "What did you bring to eat?" he asked. "Got no herbal tea or salad stuff here. Or gluten-free bread."

"Don't worry about me. I'll eat what you eat. It'll only be for a week or two. What are you having for dinner?"

"Nore's stew. There's plenty left."

"Stew? I haven't had stew in years. That'll do for me."

Phil drained his can, his eyes on his sister. *Is she letting her hair down or is she up to something? Probably planning to finish what Nore started but she can't do that if I don't trust her. Well, it's not working, sis. I don't trust you as far as I can throw you. Any of you.*

He reached for Cindy's empty can. She was looking around for somewhere to put it.

"The recycling bin is in the kitchen. If you're ready, we'll take your stuff upstairs."

"Where's your vac? I'll get rid of the dust before I make the bed. Don't want to be sneezing all night."

That sounds more like you, Phil thought. "No need," he told her. "We were talking about having a live-in home help, so I cleaned the room."

"I'm not saying you wouldn't do a good job, but well,--." She stopped talking, embarrassed.

"Suit yourself. The vac is still on the landing. I'll take up what I can manage."

He led the way up, the corner of one pillow gripped in his teeth, the other hugged against his chest under his right arm while he grabbed the stair rail with his left hand.

Cindy followed, the big box cradled in her arms. It was heavy and she was puffing by the time she reached the landing. She went into the spare room, dropped the box by the nightstand and looked around.

The afternoon sunshine streamed through the window and twinkled on the shiny frames of pictures and glass trinkets that Phil had set out on a small shelf unit. She fingered the long, silky-looking drapes that matched the comforter then, with one foot, ruffled the pile of the soft rug that covered six foot of threadbare carpet next to the bed.

"It's lovely in here," she said. "I thought, um, I expected, er, well, never mind what I expected. Did you do this yourself?"

Phil felt the color creep up his neck. "Yes." *For Elsie. If I can talk her into coming here.* He put the pillows on the end of the bed. "If we do get someone to live in, she'll want her own room. I was trying to be, er---"

"Proactive," Cindy finished for him.

"Yes."

"Wow. You've gone up in my estimation, bro."

"Thanks."

Cindy knelt beside the box, opened it, and pulled out a pair of flannelette sheets which she tossed onto the bed. Then she rummaged around until she held three DVDs in her hand.

"Take these downstairs, will you?" she said, and held them out.

"What for?"

"I want to watch one tonight."

Phil took them and glanced at the titles. *Paranormal, all of them. And Cindy knows I hate this stuff. So I'm not going to be sick. I'm going to be scared to death.*

"Sorry," he said. "We don't have a DVD player."

"You don't? Omigod." Cindy sat back on her heels.

That's put a wrench in your works, hasn't it? Now you'll have to think of something else.

"So what do you and Mom do in the evenings?"

"Play cards, watch TV, read. Mom likes puzzles."

"Oh." Cindy pulled a new pack of pillow cases out of the box. She stood up and, with her back to him, tugged at the zipper on the pack. It was stuck and she had to use her teeth.

Phil dropped the DVDs back in the box. One hit a blood-veined eyeball that squinted up at him from a grotesque rubber mask, obviously a Halloween special. It made him shudder. *And that's the something else. Yeah, that would finish me off if it came at me in the middle of the night.*

He glanced at Cindy who was busy unfolding the pillow cases. He reached down and pinched the eyeball in his fingertips then, praying his sister wouldn't hear, eased the mask out of the box, tucked it under his stiff right arm, and moved towards the door.

"While you're doing that," he said, "I'll warm up the stew." He went to his room and hid the mask in his top drawer before he limped downstairs, a determined glint in his eye. *I didn't start this game. They did. I'm just defending myself.*

195

****

Chapter Thirteen

Phil shared what was left of the stew between two bowls, and put the iron pot in the sink to soak. "Grub's up," he shouted up the stairs.

Cindy came into the kitchen rubbing her arms. "I'm cold," she complained, as she pulled a chair away from the table. "It's freezing up there. Is something wrong with your boiler?"

"Don't have one. Just baseboard electric. Landlord keeps saying he'll give us a new system but I'm not holding my breath. Mom and me, we just wear more clothes. She's got loads of bed socks if you want to borrow a pair."

"Don't your pipes freeze?"

"Sure. We've got a paraffin heater I put in the bathroom on cold nights, but it's a waste of time 'cause we have to keep a window open or else the fumes would kill us. It stinks like hell, too. I'll light it tonight, seeing you're here, but leave the door open when you go in there."

"You'll have to do better than that, Phil. You'll never get a live-in home help unless you do."

"I know. Mom's working on it. Heat's next on her agenda. She's saving up for it 'cause she doesn't want to put it on a card. Hey, quit carping. Your stew's getting cold."

Cindy bent over the bowl and sniffed. "This smells so good."

"Tastes better than it smells, too. Come on. Dig in."

They ate in silence, but it was a comfortable silence, and now and again they smiled at each other. After downing the last spoonful, Phil pushed his chair away from the table and leaned back, eyes closed, legs outstretched, left hand resting on his thigh. He was warm, comfortable and his belly was full. If it hadn't been for a tickle on his hand, he might have dozed off. He opened his eyes a smidgeon, looked down, and leapt from his chair.

An enormous stink bug crawled over his left hand. Revulsion swamped him, and he flung his hand in the air. The loathsome bug landed on its back next to Cindy's bowl, its pale legs moving like pistons.

"Eeeeeek!"

She raised her spoon and was about to slam it on the stink bug when Phil yelled, "Stop. Don't crush it. The mess!"

She bumped her chair away from the table, her face ashen.

Phil ripped a sheet off the paper towel and dropped it over the bug. Then, bending low so that he could use his right hand as well as his left, he squashed the stink bug into the paper. Crumpling it into a ball, he stumbled towards the kitchen door, but stopped when he realized he had to let go with one hand before he could twist the knob.

"I'll do it." Cindy leaned round him, pulled the door open, and backed away.

He tossed the paper ball outside and kicked the door shut. Then, as if he was preventing entry of the Walking Dead, he rammed the dead bolt home and turned the key.

They returned to the table and sank onto their chairs, trembling, chests heaving in unison.

"Omigod," Cindy said. "I thought I was going to die. I HATE those things."

"Me, too. They're so ugly, and sneaky. They come at you out of nowhere. Don't know why they get me like they do 'cause they don't bite. They're just nuisances."

He remembered Noreen's shriek when she saw the spider, and for a moment he felt guilty. But then he told himself: *That was her own fault. She shouldn't have gone mushroom picking.*

"Where did that bug come from?" Cindy asked, her hand patting her still-heaving bosom.

"Outside. When it gets too cold for them, they crawl in the cracks of window frames and look for somewhere warm."

"No fear of them coming in the bedroom, then. It's colder than outside up there."

"There's worse things than stink bugs," Phil said, recalling the gruesome mask lying under his pile of tee shirts. *I'd better not scare her tonight. Not after that fright. Tomorrow, maybe.*

He collected the bowls, put them on the draining board, and ran the faucet, fluttering the fingers of his left hand in the stream of water until it was warm enough.

Cindy reached for the towel hanging on the handle of the oven. "This is nice and warm," she said, and held the bunched-up towel to her cheek. "The stove's on. What's cooking?"

"Nothing. Mom keeps it on all winter so we've got at least one warm room."

"Your gas bill must be sky high."

"It's not too bad. And it's worth it."

"So what are you going to do with yourself tonight," Cindy asked a few minutes later, as if she felt uncomfortable with the silence that had fallen.

"Probably watch *Law and Order* in the front room."

"I'll stay in here, in the warm. I've got my Kindle."

****

The Kindle died and Cindy hadn't brought her charger. Annoyed with herself, and with no-one to talk to because Phil was still glued to the TV, she went to bed and spent the next hour texting Trev or playing Candy Crush on her phone.

She gave up playing and sat up in bed, her knees drawn up, the hood of her robe over her head. Her fingers were freezing and she tucked her hands inside her sleeves. She glanced at the little alarm clock on the nightstand. Ten thirty. Is that all it is?

God, I'm cold, even in my bath robe and Mom's bed socks. Dunno how Phil stands it. Poor guy. He's had a rotten life but he never complains. He doesn't deserve to die. There's no need for him to be bumped off, anyway, not now Mom's back on her feet. If Al and Nore still want him dead, they'll have to do it themselves. I'm taking no more part in their stupid plan.

She heard Phil's uneven tread as he came up the stairs. She hadn't closed her door fully and light glowed through the crack after he switched on the bathroom light. There was a tap when the toilet seat fell against the tank. She heard him piddling, and then a short flush. Silence for a few seconds, and then a click, followed by a whumph. He must have lit the old heater.

The glow through the door grew momentarily brighter, but then it faded, and Cindy heard him climbing upstairs.

"'Night, Phil," she called, when she judged he had reached his room.

"'Night, Cin," he called back.

She switched off the bedside lamp, drew her robe closer around her, curled into a ball, and snuggled into the covers. It took her a while before she stopped shivering. Eventually warmth, blessed warmth, surrounded her. Sleep beckoned.

Then she realized she had to pee.

She clenched her thighs together, but her bladder demanded immediate relief. Unwillingly, she unwound the covers, flicked on the lamp, and tiptoed over the landing to the bathroom. In the doorway she trod on the front of her lopsided robe, pitched forward, and crashed into the heater. It toppled sideways against the bath, onto the thin towel that hung over its side.

****

Phil heard the racket. He tumbled out of bed and hobbled down to the landing, to be greeted by smoke pouring out of the bathroom.

Flames from the burning towel had crept up the plastic shower curtain, melting it, causing the black smoke. The fumes made Phil heave. The bath rug was alight, and so was a heap of clothes lying in the doorway. What were they doing there?

Jeez! Not clothes! Cindy!

He grabbed one foot with his left hand and tugged her half-way onto the landing.

She screamed. Her long hair was burning.

Phil fumbled to unbutton his pajama top, intending to beat her with it, but stopped when Cindy screamed again. He had to get her out of the bathroom.

He bent double so that he could use both hands, the cast weighing heavily on his arm. Awkwardly, he tugged his sister's feet until he'd dragged her, upside down, up the stairs. Blood rushed into his head while he fought to keep himself from falling on top of her, but eventually he reached the top landing. There he rolled her around to smother any remaining sparks. Pain shot down his bad arm. The cast had cracked. He sat down beside Cindy and nursed his arm.

She looked a sorry sight. Her singed hair stuck to her blackened face. Tears had washed clean lines on her cheeks and down her neck.

"Omigod, Phil. What are we going to do?" she wailed, bursting into tears again.

The carpet on the landing below them was alight. Flames licked the wooden bannister and raced past Betsy's room towards the spare room, creating a fiery barrier between the attic and downstairs. Then the flames sprang onto the attic stairs, and the heat and stink of the growing inferno surged towards them.

"We're trapped!" shrieked Cindy.

"Maybe not."

Phil grabbed her hand and pulled her into his room. Once inside, he slammed the door, hoping it would delay the progress of the flames. But he slammed too hard. The door fell crookedly off its hinges and bumped down the stairs, blocking them and adding fuel to the fire.

Cindy screamed again.

"SHUT UP! Help me open this window!"

He pushed the bottom half up as high as it would go, and used his head as a prop while he dislodged the piece of wood holding up the top half. Then he jerked his head away.

Both sections of the sash window slid down. The upper one toppled outwards and crash-landed on the porch roof. Then Phil swung his bedside chair at the lower pane. It and the chair disappeared through the gaping hole in the wall, and the sound of breaking glass again echoed through the night.

Phil turned to Cindy. "Come on. You first."

"Where?"

"Out the window. Onto the porch roof. Quick, before we're toast."

"But there's broken glass down there."

Phil seized his bedding and tossed that onto the porch roof, too. Then he helped Cindy climb backwards out of the window. She clung to the sill while fire crept into the bedroom.

"Let go! Let go!"

"I daren't," she sobbed.

He felt the heat behind him. This was no time for gentle persuasion. He pushed her hands away, and she fell, landing flat on her back on the porch roof. He heard more breaking glass, followed by high-pitched screams from Cindy.

He scrambled through the window after her, then realized that, if he let go, he would land on top of his sister and probably cripple her.

He hung like a bat from the creaking window sill in the freezing air, while pain throbbed through him. The right sleeve of his thick pajamas snagged on Alan's hook and took the weight of his right arm. He was wearing his singlet under his pajamas, but neither gave him any protection. The cold numbed his fingers and froze the sweat on his chest. He pushed his bare toes against the siding, trying to distribute the weight. Then everything went numb – his brain, his arms, his feet, everything.

From a long way away, he heard sirens and bells clanging. The sounds grew louder, interspersed with excited shouts from the street below. Suddenly, a sea of colored lights spread around the house and the pulse of sirens woke his heart. At first it pumped in tempo with them, but soon raced ahead. The pain woke up too, and he realised he couldn't hold on any longer.

A heavy gloved hand pressed on his back. Then it slid round his waist and tugged his body into the cab of a swaying cherry-picker, right next to him.

"Let go." The voice came from a helmeted head beside him.

A whoosh of orange flame billowed from the gaping opening above them. Almost simultaneously, a plume of water from below doused it. Freezing water splashed onto Phil, and he sank to the floor of the cab. Needles of pain stabbed his right arm.

"Ouch!"

"What's up?"

"My arm's broke."

"We'll see to it, soon as we're out of here."

The cherry-picker swayed away from the house.

Phil struggled to his knees and looked down to the porch.

"My sister. My sister fell on the porch roof. Is she all right?"

"We've got her. Taken her to Matthews. You're going there, too."

$$****$$

Chapter Fourteen

Early the next morning, at the height of the morning rush hour, Noreen took Jinja for a run in the nearby park before she left for work. She had hoped that Joe would do the honors, but he disclaimed responsibility.

"No way. You said you'd look after the brute. I'm off to work."

Fifteen minutes later, cars screeched to a halt while, on the end of a long lead, a huge lean and sinewy greyhound swerved in and out of the traffic.

Noreen pounded behind it, both hands clasped into the handle of the retractable lead.

"Stop, Jinja! Stop!" she yelled.

The animal made a sudden dash towards a lamp post on the sidewalk where a terrier cocked its leg. Its owner stood close to it, purple plastic bag in hand, ready to poop scoop.

The swift, unexpected change of direction yanked Noreen off her feet. She fell heavily, the lead entangled round her hands. It sliced through her gloves, and fire shot through the fingers of her left hand. The pain stopped. Momentarily numbed, she hung grimly onto the lead's handle and was dragged face down across the gritty road and between the enormous wheels of a Peterbilt truck that had stopped because the rest of the traffic had stopped.

Meanwhile, Jinja reached the terrier, and sniffed its hind quarters.

The little dog yapped at the greyhound. Its owner bent to grab hold of its collar, but missed, and the dogs circled each other, jaws wide open, both ready to get in the first bite.

Noreen scrambled on hands and knees out from under the tractor-trailer, her unfeeling hands letting go of the handle. The lead zipped back to Jinja and the handle clouted the terrier's owner hard behind her knees. She toppled over, her legs became entangled in both leads, and she fell onto the sidewalk. Her glasses flew off, to be crushed under the wheels of a passing cyclist who had decided to escape the hold-up on the road by riding on the path.

The screams of both women, the terrier's yapping and Jinja's deep barks joined the honking of cars and parps of trucks. It was bedlam.

Somebody must have called the cops. Flashing lights appeared out of nowhere. Sirens, the wails of an ambulance and the hoarse honks of a fire engine added to the din.

The terrier's owner scrambled to her feet and was trying to separate her Charlie from Jinja. She was helped by the Peterbilt driver who had jumped down from his cab. He unclipped the terrier's lead, and the woman scooped Charlie up into her arms. The trucker swung a boot at Jinja who'd leapt at the scared woman, his massive front claws cutting through her jacket.

The agony of two broken fingers wormed into Noreen's consciousness, and she screamed louder. Her scream attracted the attention of a cop who was threading his way between the cars. He turned towards a paramedic following close behind him. "Over here!" he shouted and pointed at the group at the lamp post.

Recognition dawned when he reached Noreen. "I know you," he said. "You're, you're..."

"Noreen Dawtry. You came to Mom's house the other day."

"You don't need me." The trucker jumped back into his vehicle, unwilling to be involved any further in the incident.

Sergeant Palmer let him go after ascertaining that no-one but Noreen and the terrier's owner had suffered damage, and the traffic moved on.

Meanwhile, another officer tied Jinja to the lamp post.

"You've got a dangerous animal there!" Charlie's owner shouted. "It oughta be put down."

"He's not mine," wept Noreen. "I'm just looking after him while Alan's in hospital." She nursed her left hand. "Oh, my god, it hurts." she sobbed.

"Let's get you to Matthews." A paramedic went to lead her towards the ambulance.

"But what about Jinja?"

Sergeant Palmer pulled out his radio. "Get K9 here," he said into it. Then he turned to Noreen. "Your name again, and address?"

"Noreen Dawtry. 64 Winslow Gardens."

"Go with the medic, ma'am. We'll come to Matthews and take a full statement from you after the dog's been taken to the pound."

****

Chapter Fifteen

Theo stared at Noreen in disbelief when the paramedics led her into Emergency.

"You, too!" she exclaimed. "What's going on with your family?"

Half-a-dozen newsmen had congregated near the exit. They rushed towards Noreen, yelling questions at her, while the paramedics shielded her.

"What happened?"

"Is your sister going to make it?"

"What about your brother?"

205

Noreen wiped tears away with her grimy right hand. During the drive to Matthews, the paramedics had strapped her left arm, and the cream-colored sling looked unbelievably pristine against the mud and blood on her jacket.

"What the heck are you talking about?"

While the reporters' attention was on Noreen, Theo dug out her phone from her pocket. Then, holding the instrument between her ear and shoulder, she fished sheets of paper out of plastic trays on her desk.

"Jermyn?" Theo said into the phone, "the other sister's here. Been in an accident by the looks of it. I'll call you with the full story soon as I can."

She dropped the phone back into her pocket and pushed the papers towards Noreen.

"Here, fill in your details."

Noreen pointed to the sling. "I can't. I'm left-handed. What are they talking about?" She jerked her head towards the reporters.

"You mean you don't know? Cindy's in the Burns Unit. Phil's being treated for minor burns and smoke inhalation, plus having his arm reset. Your Mom's house burned down last night."

"Omigod. Really?"

"Gospel. Look, I'm busy. I'm on my own here. What happened to you?"

"My hand's killing me. I think I've broke it." Tears trickled down Noreen's cheeks.

"She was involved in a dog fight," one of the paramedics said.

Theo's head shot up. "How long since you had a rabies shot?"

"Is that your blood or the dog's?" A reporter pushed his phone in front of Noreen.

"Where was the fight?" another asked.

"Get out of here! All of you!" bawled Theo. "Get out of here before I call the police."

The door swung open to admit Sergeant Palmer and another officer. The reporters stood aside to let them approach the desk.

"We're here to take a statement from Mrs. Dawtry," the policeman said to Theo.

"Mrs. Dawtry." "Mrs. Dawtry." Noreen's name was whispered into smartphones.

"What's going on in here?"

The Hospital Administrator seemed to materialize out of nowhere. He stood in the middle of Emergency, his face grim. "What's all this commotion?" he called. "This is a hospital. Not a place of public amusement. Anyone not related to this patient needs to leave immediately."

The newsmen reluctantly edged towards the exit.

"Except you, of course," the Administrator added, nodding at the police officers.

"We'll wait outside in the car until Mrs. Dawtry has been attended to," Sergeant Palmer said. "Let us know when she's ready and we'll drive her to the station to take her statement."

"That would be helpful," the Administrator said.

Sergeant Palmer addressed Noreen. "Is there anyone you want us to contact?"

"Oh, yes. My boss. And Joe, my husband. He's at work, but he can come and pick me up."

"We'll drive you home when we're done at the station, ma'am. What are their numbers?"

****

The best part of an hour elapsed before an orderly guided Noreen towards the police car.

Sergeant Palmer opened the back door and helped her inside. He was settling himself in his seat beside the driver when a black car drove into the parking lot and parked near them.

"Might have known he'd turn up," Noreen said.

Both cops turned to watch Jermyn lock his car door and head towards Emergency.

The driver swatted Sergeant Palmer against his chest with the back of his hand.

"Wily Willy. Wily Willy," he said, excitedly, and craned forward. "We got him!"

"You sure, Scott?" Sergeant Palmer sounded skeptical.

"Wily Willy?" Noreen's laugh resounded in the back of the car. "That's Jermyn Tredigan, chairman of ASOT."

"Told yer!" Scott punched the air. "Let's go get 'im."

"Hold your horses, pal." Sergeant Palmer swiveled round to face Noreen. "You're dead certain that's Tredigan?"

"Positive. Why?"

"We know him as William Nesbitt. Drug dealer and money launderer. We've been after him for months, but he keeps slipping through the net."

"He's coming out!" Scott pointed at the entrance to ER.

Tredigan skipped lightly down the steps, looking towards his car.

"He'll get away again," Scott yelled. "Come on. Let's go, Joe."

Both cops leapt out of the car, leaving the doors swinging, and moved towards Tredigan.

He saw them coming and ran to his car, but they reached him first. Scott dragged the suspect's hands behind his back, while Sergeant Palmer snapped on handcuffs. Then he stepped back and said something to Tredigan that Noreen couldn't hear.

"You've got the wrong man," Jermyn protested, while the sergeant guided him to the police car and pushed him into the back seat. "Never heard of ASOT. Whatever it is, I've got nothing to do with it. I'll sue you for wrongful arrest."

Noreen leaned towards him. "Well, look who it ain't," she said, feigning surprise. "Fancy meeting you here, Mr. Tredigan. Making another of your hospital visits, eh? Who did you come to check on this time? Phil? Or Cindy? She's in a bad way. Nasty burns."

Tredigan stared at her, open-mouthed.

"You remember me, don't you? Noreen Dawtry. Betsy Henderson's daughter. Your first big winner. Six thousand bucks a week for life. And we've had naught but grief since. It's all your fault."

"You!" Tredigan spat. "The stroppy one."

"Ah, you do remember me. We had a lively, er, discussion in your office, didn't we?"

"He's our man all right," Sergeant Palmer said. He nudged Scott. "Let's go."

****

On arrival at the police station, a Detective Sergeant led Jermyn into an interview room. Noreen stood watching until the door closed behind them.

"What will happen to him?" she asked Sergeant Palmer. "Will he go to jail?"

"Not straight away. We don't normally do that for a white-collar offence. We'll interview him, charge him with fraud and set a date and time for a court appearance, and then release him on bail."

"Who'll bail him out? His company?"

"No. It'll be on his personal recognizance. That means he must promise to appear in court on a given date and time after providing personal bail of, say, twenty thousand bucks."

"What's to stop him vamoosing the minute he leaves here?"

"If he's been known to travel, he'll have to surrender his passport. And if he doesn't turn up in court, the personal bail turns into a cash bail. He'll lose the twenty thousand."

"What d'you think will happen to Mom's six thousand a week?"

Sergeant Palmer shook his head. "Forget it. She won't get any more from Wily Willy. But I didn't bring you here to talk about him. It's time you made that statement."

****

Chapter Sixteen

Phil was discharged from hospital the following weekend. He stood on the steps outside ER, waiting for someone from the landlord's office to give him a lift to his old home where he planned to pick up a few items.

Elsie stood beside him, ready to bid him goodbye. "Where are ye and yer Ma goin' ter live?" she asked. "I heard the old hoose is no safe. That it will have ter be pulled down."

"We'll be at Alan's until the landlord finds us a new place," he said. "Mom will stay here a couple more days while I tidy it up. It's a tip right now. I've got to go home first, though, and grab whatever I can. Good job I kept all the important stuff – policies, bank books – in a deed box under the stairs. They won't be damaged."

A car pulled up in front of them, "Paradise Properties" painted on its side.

"Time to go," Phil said.

Elsie reached for him and gave him a hug.

210

He held her tight for as long as he dared. "Keep me posted about Cindy, won't you," he said. "You've got my number."

"Aye, laddie. I will."

****

Phil stared at his old home. Gaunt blackened rafters held up what was left of the roof. They had patches of blue sky showing between them. The second floor was mostly gutted, too. Amazingly, the first floor and porch appeared relatively unharmed. His ancient rocker stood in its old position, its cushion undisturbed on the seat.

"Don't try going upstairs," the guy from Paradise Properties warned.

"As if," Phil muttered.

"Give me a buzz when you're ready, and I'll take you and whatever stuff you salvage to your brother's. See you."

The car pulled away and Phil let himself into the front room.

Nothing in the cupboard under the stairs was damaged. Phil used his feet to nudge the deed box towards the front door. Once it was out on the porch, he returned to collect tins of beans, soup and vegetables from the kitchen, plus everything hanging on the coat rack, and piled them on the porch, too.

It was slow hard work, and he needed a drink. The power had been turned off, but the cans in the bottom drawer of the fridge were cool to the touch. He took one out to the porch, sat down in his rocker, and took a long pull.

His arm twitched involuntarily and beer spilled onto his pants. He knew what was coming. He'd been in this situation too many times. Sure enough, his heart fluttered, and then started beating wildly. The familiar pain tightened his chest and blood pounded in his ears.

Take it easy, he thought. It would be truly ironic if, after defeating his siblings' efforts to bump him off, he did himself in.

211

Even more ironic now that there was no more money coming from ASOT to spur them on.

In a way, he was grateful to them. If they hadn't tried to kill him, he would never have met Elsie.

Ah, Elsie. Just the thought of her made his heart race.

He tried to put her out of his mind, but then gave up the effort.

Might as well live dangerously and die happy when it's time to go.

He settled down in his rocker and dreamed of Elsie.

THE END

ACKNOWLEDGMENTS

As will be apparent to most of you, I wrote the stories in this book over a long period of time. Who remembers transcribing dictation that had been recorded on a tiny cassette tape, or fighting to open an obstinate sash window? During the eighty-one years that I have been alive, I have seen so many changes – from calculators the size of shoeboxes reduced to wafer-thin products that don't have to be plugged in; cars that cannot be mended by the owner and which are guided from an unseen voice in the sky; coverage of games on television that can be halted and rings and arrows instantly marked on the screen; etc., etc..

Throughout those years, I've been fortunate in having special people around me who have helped me. It began with my teachers at school in England, continued with the several mentors and instructors who critiqued my early attempts, and, of course, my dear family have supported me every step of the way.

Among these very special people are Taffy Cannon, my mentor while I studied with LongRidge Writers; Paul Swearingen, sadly now passed away, our beloved modulator on the *Writer's Digest* Forum; "updog" and "wednesday", "laycrew" and "rob the third", "shadow-walker" and "warren" – all members of that forum; Paula Berenstein (formerly of *The Writing Show* fame and now the author of the *Amanda Lester Detective* series) for her help, advice and encouragement, freely given while I wrote my *"Martian Missions"* sci-fi series. Most recently, Sergeant Pettingill of Dover Police set me right on matters of police procedure in the novella that ended the book *"Fumbled Fratricide"*.

I hope you have enjoyed reading these stories. If you have comments on any of them, please feel free to drop me a line on <u>drthypiper@yahoo.com</u> or post a review on the site where you bought the book. Thank you.

Other books by Dorothy Piper:

The *Martian Missions* series

The Gift

Staying Alive

Pick Your Planet

The last book in the series (**One Man's Plans**)
should be available in 2019.

Piper Love Stories, Parts I and II
Four generations of James Piper's descendants
from 1783 to 1970

And written under pen-name Jodi Havel:

Truth Will Out

Brotherly Love

Made in the USA
Columbia, SC
24 July 2018